Is That So

a novel by

Patrick McCarthy

Is That So

People aren't so easily understood. You can't predict which way they'll go. What they'll say next. Riley understood this years ago. Even as a boy he stopped inventing prepared speeches. They never worked out.

But he was no longer a boy. And that was the issue. If people were mysteries to him, it was also true that he'd become a mystery to himself.

If he wrote about his boyhood it'd be a biography. He was a stranger, a foreigner. A dead person. That boy he once was.

And this was true of other people in his life that he'd known for many years. They became something else. Sometimes two-dimensional, like cartoons. Or, rarely, four or five dimensional. Myths. Ghosts. Saints. Archetypes.

He didn't have many illusions about the people in his world. But, really, what was his world anyway? It was nothing but people. Present ones, absent ones.

People against a dim, shadowy background. When he remembered his world it was never a natural setting, or a neighborhood, with buildings, trees, clouds, streets, rivers or oceans. It was just a face, two eyes, a moving silhouette.

It was midnight, and he fired off a birthday greeting to Eva. She was on the other coast and she'd be able to read it first thing in the morning. He was sure she was in bed by now, and asleep. She was not the type to toss and turn. An anxious woman, but of a different order than the insomniacs. Like Inga. Or even Rebecca.

Women. If you really were accurate about it, Riley's world was women, and nothing else.

It was hard to dwell on men. There was nothing to learn from them.

He must have been in a sweetly melancholy mood. He typed the birthday greetings, edited them for clarity, and simplicity. Decided to be a bit more personal. Somewhat idiosyncratic. Read the text over five or six times and sent it off.

Eva was older. Not old, like Riley. There was an age gap. Twenty-one years. It seemed huge at one time. But no longer. She was a grandmother now. It sounds funny to call her a grandmother even though he had these very erotic memories of her. And fairly recently.

The vanished boy in him would have been shocked. That Riley, as an old man, could still feel sexual passion for a woman. A grandmother, no less. That boy would have been depressed and maybe even disgusted. He couldn't have understood. He would have drawn an ugly caricature of the whole situation.

Eva was the single remaining erotic memory that he had. Or actually had him. All the other women from back then were either dead, dying, or faded into nothingness.

Or course, there were other ones who existed in the present. Some of them close by in Los Angeles, where he lived. They bought his paintings. Came into the gallery, or to the studio. He had some pretty earthy feelings about some of them. He was still a man. A vigorous male of the species. Sort of.

Eva sent him brief texts on his birthday, and he did the same for her. They never talked or saw each other. Not for at least six years. Maybe more. Time was different today for Riley, and maybe even for her.

Time was like a motor being turned on. It started slowly, but gradually, irresistibly revved up, and eventually ten years went by like one year.

Time was also like a violent crash where a car tumbled over and over and by centrifugal force threw all the occupants out of windows.

You couldn't hold onto anything from your past. It was whirled away and you were left alone with your peaceful thoughts staring up at the starry sky.

Time was a wet dog shaking the water off until it felt dry.

You could say a lot about time and it wouldn't be that far-fetched. People would agree, some of them.

He called Eva in the morning, like he said he would.

It was later in the day for her.

"Hello, Riley."

"How's your day going?" He had already wished her happy birthday, in the text.

"My day? Busy. Can you call me tomorrow? I'm over at Bella's."

Riley could hear noise in the background. Bella was her daughter.

"Sure."

"Can you call me in the morning?"

"All right. Enjoy yourself."

He imagined a longer talk, but then again, it was so like Eva. She always had something to distract her. Riley wondered if

Eva was nothing more than a distracted being. Busy with this or that, endlessly. The opposite of himself.

Also, whether or not he was more superfluous to her than she was to him. It was difficult to judge. But, looking at it from the most objective angle, he decided that she was still more to him than he was to her. He often said that, and she just as often argued against it. In the way of busy, distracted people. Also, she was still quite attractive. Pretty much any man would agree. But this was also merely his projections at work.

He logged on and noticed that she'd already sent him a few photos. She was blowing out the candles on a birthday cake. Surrounded by three small kids. Her grandchildren.

"This is what my day is like." She wrote. "I look forward to talking tomorrow!"

Riley rubbed his chin and began to reflect on the whole thing. What was the point?

Eva had her world on the East Coast. Riley had his world in Los Angeles. She flew out there several times. He never returned to her city. The city where they first met. And what were the chances of that ever happening? Nil. He had no intention of revisiting that burg. That hicktown, as he called it.

Not to Eva's face. To her it was home. He loathed everything about it. Except Eva. And a few friends. And, of course, Rebecca, who still owned her house there.

But for Riley it was tempting stack of firewood. He wanted to light a match to his memories. To watch them roar into flames as he danced around it like a naked Indian. To wipe them from his mind for good.

He was a painter. And a painter was no painter if he was imprisoned by the past. Or the future. A painter had better focus on the present. And paint from the vantage point of what is happening right now. Hadn't he understood it yet? The stubborn idiot.

Another day went by. He called her, and the same thing happened. She was in the middle of something. She'd call him tomorrow, all right? Sure. Of course.

It was time for the periodic conflagration that destroyed one world and gave birth to a new one. Some kind of an old Greek believed. Heraclitus, one of Riley's first heroes.

For this ancient thinker everything was in flux. Very fluid, but more like a fire than a flowing stream. But fire turned everything into a melted down motion.

It all changes. Accept that. Live it. Only a small hard seed remains what it is, but everything else is moving, growing, shrinking, waxing and waning.

Riley was fine with that. What was holding him back from the Heraclitan flow? From the consuming fire that freed him from what was over and done? Nothing. Or maybe it was a nothingness that had some secret life at its core. Nothingness that concealed something that wouldn't easily vanish and become utterly extinguished.

Raphael, his grandson, walked into the studio. He was eleven and could now go outdoors by himself, roaming the streets of Boyle Heights. At least within a few block radius. He loved the few retail businesses. The comic book shop, the Mexican convenience store. The people liked seeing him. He wasn't shy. He spoke right up and made his point.

Riley kept examining his life. How it went from this to that. From the Midwest to Los Angeles, with some side trips. He had a hard time seeing it as something substantial and real. It felt arbitrary and rootless. Not like his old hometown, where

generations, stayed and were satisfied with themselves. Too much running around wasn't for them.
Too much change was ridiculous.

"I want to tell you a historical fact," Raphael said. "Would you like to hear it?"

"Well, certainly." Riley stopped what he was doing and turned to face his grandson.

"In the beginning, Batman wore gloves and had a gun."

"Is that right? Let me think if can remember."

"Batman, and the other superheroes, first appeared right before the World War started. In 1939."

"That makes sense. America needed some heroes to fight the bad guys."

"Yes. The Nazis."

"But they weren't called superheroes in those days. I don't remember what we called them. Let me look it up. Oh. They were known as adventure heroes. With super powers."

"Batman doesn't have superpowers."

"Yes. But he uses technology." Riley thought about that signal in the sky.

"Right. Gadgetry."

Gadgetry. Hah.

His grandson was deeply into this fictional world. More than Riley was at his age, but he often repeated the facts of his own childhood, always adding a few new ones. Raphael listened, but he had his own ideas. Riley's didn't seem to catch hold of the boy's imagination. But you could never tell. Sometimes he'd surprise the old man by mentioning something that originated with Riley. So he listened to him after all.

As a boy Riley was too easily influenced by external forces. Everything interested him. He was highly curious. But this had some negative consequences. He was too aware of whatever was out there, but less so about what was inside his own brain. It ended up making him less original. More like a sponge. Instead of an erupting volcano. Definitely not a chunk of uranium. Something that absorbed, instead of radiating.

Raphael radiated from his own nature. Giving off his own kind of glow. People weren't sure what to make of it. His mother seemed most comfortable with it. She loved him exactly as he is, was, or will be.

Later in life the reverse motion set in for Riley. He began to empty himself. To express himself from whatever he had gathered along the way. But most of this was merely a version of what came from outside. Not really that uniquely his own. He now tried to reach down to that part of him that actually did the gathering. What was it? Who was it? That being who was so curious, so obsessed.

"How many books do you have about the Holocaust?" Raphael asked.

"Around three hundred."

"Did you read them all?"

"Yes. Every one."

The facts of World War 2 were intersecting with the invention of superheroes. This insight was something new for Raphael. And it was only cursorily interpreted by his grandfather.

Riley knew that American propaganda rose to the challenge during that period. The artists did their part. A democratic American Superman was needed in order to crush the Neitzschean myth of the Aryan ubermensch. Hitler wanted an army of supermen but instead he ended up with a gang of depraved submen.

Riley wondered how much his grandson would be able to understand this truth. He was still too young. And perhaps his father was slanting him along other lines. Slowing down the boy's eventual realizations. But not preventing them from someday being grasped.

How much importance was a grandfather supposed to have? It was vague, uncertain. It depended on so many various and competing influences. Riley's grandfather loomed large, even today. Maybe because his father was absent for much of the time. Traveling out of town to oversee the construction projects.

His mother's father was a self-made, self-educated man. A poor boy who made good. Who married a German beauty and raised six children. A great example of a man. Riley was a bit of a crank by comparison. A lone wolf artist.

Riley's other grandfather, Riley O'Kerry the First, who the grandson was named after, was perhaps an even bigger influence. Even though he died before Riley was born.

The original Riley emigrated to the States from Ireland at the end of the 19th century. A penniless youth of seventeen. By age fifty he was a millionaire with nine children, living in a mansion. The American dream come true.

But the grandson's dreams were quite different from the grandfather, in Riley's case. Both grandfathers. The third generation Amerians were unlike their immigrant ancestors. Different goals, different drives, different values. A new breed, in many cases.

Riley saw it in Los Angeles. And before that in other areas of the States. How Americans changed over time. But not completely. They still carried traces of the old country.

"Riley isn't really that American," said Colleen, his Irish sister-in-law. "He's more like my brothers."

And he'd have to agree, without knowing Colleen's brothers. He didn't feel that American. The transplantation was only successful to a degree. There was something of the Irish rogue about him. A bit of a gypsy tinker, a moody scholar buried in his obscure books, dabbling in mysticism, and slathering paint on his throwaway canvases.

If this was primeval Irish, or even druidic, it might explain a lot about Riley. A solitary at heart, dreamy, idealistic, rebellious, anti-clerical, unconstrained, ultra-individualistic. He was modern only in the sense that he loathed any tradition from the past.

"You know what PoMo is, don't you?" Professor Manny asked Riley at dinner last year.

"Yes."

Post-modern. But Manny left it that. Riley had some ideas about post-modern, and no doubt Manny had plenty to say about this development. But they moved on to other subjects.

Did Riley see himself as a postmodern whatever? A postmodern painter, or postmodern novelist? Well, in a way, yes. If postmodern was the antithesis of modern. If it was a critical, analytical assessment of modernism. A break from modernism, as if it was no longer worthy of continuing. Ignoring modernism as if it never happened.

This idea struck him with intensified force last night as he was reading a novel by a Latin American author. "The Green House" by Mario Vargas Llosa. A thick, complicated piece of writing. Not exactly Finnegan's Wake, but maybe a South American version. At least in some parts. Earlier chapters.

Modernism was a willingness to destroy traditional structures in all forms of art. To try anything. What the hell, why not? And it had its triumphs, but also many defeats.

The novel he was reading attempted something like interlaced dialogue, where two different conversations were going at once, sentence by sentence.

It was annoying. Maybe it was brilliant. But tiresome. Riley grew impatient, ready to fling the book aside. But he continued, and it seemed as if the author also started to question his technique and used it sparingly in the final chapters.

Postmodernism had some real advantages. It was straightforward. It abandoned some ill-considered conceits of those who immediately went before them. Or it swallowed them up and turned them into a kind of amalgamated synthesis. You could now incorporate bits and pieces of modernism in your latest efforts. And call it postmodern.

Riley had a fresh take on the situation. Always desirable. But also some new doubts.

Was he already thinking of post-postmodernism? He wouldn't be the first person to have that notion.

But it was something else that bothered him. You saw it everyday in Los Angeles. This idea of never giving up. Not quitting. Endless urging to keep at it. Keep swinging away at the problem. At your anonymity. At your failures.

It got under his skin. Quitting had a bad reputation. Undeservedly so. Why butt your skull against a steel door that won't open? Quit doing dumb shit. Try something new. There are other paths available.

"I'm almost finished with "One Hundred Years of Solitude," Kristina said. "It's an awesome book. I loved it."

"I'm also reading a South American writer. It's good that we check out other novelists beside our favorites." By this Riley meant the French and Russian greats.

"It is. I especially like the way Marquez talks about love. And how money and love never mix."

"I don't remember that part, but it does sound good. I must have been influenced by his ideas. I do recall one scene where a man is about to be executed and he says something like 'he realized that those he hated most, he loved most.' It was a startling comment. I had to rethink a lot about my life."

"I like that remark, too. It reminded me of how I feel about Rainer. Marquez writes well about sexuality, too."

"Right. Latin writers seem to acknowledge something jungly about sex."

"Jungly. They talk about having sex for days. Not just a few minutes. A very passionate culture. Not European."

"Or North American, either. A big reason why I think American writers are so dull and superficial. Because of their sexual style. It must go back to Puritan times."

Riley didn't even try to write about sex. In all its details. He wasn't up to the job. He was not only American, which is bad enough, but Irish, on top of it. Talk about a squeamish set of genes. He was lucky to even know what to do with his prick.

"And the poet. Neruda. He's also good when writing about sex."

"He is."

"But I really liked how Marquez discussed the impossibility of true love existing when money was taken into account. How it ruined all true love. It's why people experience true love when they're young and poor. After that it's extremely unlikely because they acquire a taste for money. Which kills true love."

"If either of the two, the man or the woman, has money on their mind, then true love is nearly impossible. That's been my experience."

"Not only is money in the way, but I'm finding out that these men I've been meeting are mostly held back by past loves. They can't move forward."

"Something else that gets in the way of true love. The past and money."

Riley had his own difficulties with both obstacles. If a woman loved money more than she loved him, it wrecked everything between them. He'd never be rich. He refused to bow down before the dollar. He wanted the bare necessities but nothing more. Luxuries only got in the way of his creativity.

He was surprised that his daughter now sang the same tune. But actually her mother wasn't that fascinated by wealth either. Not to the degree that it overrode other desires. And the same was true of Rebecca's family. Her father was an old-fashioned healer, a surgeon who concentrated on his patients, and not their payments.

Riley's indifference to excessive capital must have come from somewhere. His father always was alarmed at his son's "communist" tendencies. He couldn't figure out why the boy was that way. How Riley preferred getting a summer job instead of golfing everyday at the country club. How he shared his lunch money with a poor black student. How his girl friends came from the wrong side of town.

But Riley's mother and father came from a line of Catholics who always took care of the poor. They believed the words of the Sermon on the Mount. This type of Catholic is no longer much in evidence. Not like the old days, when the Irish were the immigrant class in America. The Irish had advanced from prizefighters to politicians. And become upper middle class. And many were now arch-conservatives.

"I'd like to ask the next guy I meet if he'd be willing to live in a single empty room with me. Wouldn't our love be enough?" Kristina asked.

"I've always believed it would be. Extra money in the bank never increased the love between myself and a woman. And as far as the past goes, that might be an even more daunting impediment to true love."

"I'm surprised to learn that men are so hung up on their exes. I even talked about it with Michael Baker. I said that's enough about our former lovers. Let's talk about us. Let's stick to the present. But he couldn't do it. He kept babbling on about his ex-wife, or the woman he had a child with. He couldn't free himself from her. And this was also the case with Philippe."

"So this inability to escape the past is beyond gender. Men have as much trouble as women in this area."

"I'm becoming convinced of it."

"But what does it mean? Really. To me it means that you still want sex from a person from your past. When that completely dies then that particular past dies with it. I tried to kill my desires for Eva with my attraction to Inga. But it didn't work."

"It did for awhile. When you were really involved with her."

"Right. But it didn't work because it's probably always wrong to use one person to replace another person. People shouldn't be used as a means to an end. They're ends in themselves."

"But you've always said that a new love destroys an old love."

"Only if the old love is weak and dying, or actually dead."

"So it takes time for an old love to die. That's why being alone for a period is important."

"It seems to help. But an old love is really dead when you no longer want sex from a person from your past and now only want sex from a new person."

All of this seemed true, but somewhat abstract also. It was more theoretical than real. It was something that Riley had learned but he was now prepared to learn more. He needed to learn more if he wanted to improve.

"I can't stand that thing they hold in the Nevada desert each year," he said. "Burning Man festival. I'm so glad I'll never attend such it. I see all these photos on Instagram of people wandering about wearing costumes. At the end they light these large sculptures on fire. Like some ancient rite, I suppose. But I'm forced to agree with one person's explanation. The huge fire is like burning away your past. Getting rid of things that are hanging you up. That sounds good to me."

"It sounds good to me, also."

"And because of our talks, and our experiences, I now see another issue that I hadn't noticed before. Especially for you. The older men are bogged down and hindered by the traces of previous lovers and wives. The young men don't have that much holding them back, but they're also raw and naive and you don't see much of a future with them. So for you the young mean no future, and the old are enslaved by the past."

"So no true love from young or old men but for different reasons?"

"Well, each will have their respective challenges for you."

"True love only exists between two people."

"Right. It's a doorway that is only big enough for two. And no one else. Young men might have no women on their mind but they could have and will have in the future.   Old men will be obsessed with one person in their past."

"Sounds dreary. How can true love happen under such circumstances?"

"It can, and it does. But it's rare, like we say."

They were quiet for a time. Then Riley spoke once again.

"Let me see if I can get it right. A young man because he hasn't really been in love is unpredictable and undependable. An old man because he has been in love is fixated on a single previous love."

"So neither are able to fully live in the present with a woman."

"It seems to be the case. Each will have particular handicaps. Which prevents true love from blossoming. But it's never impossible. Only unlikely."

Riley was speaking mostly about himself and how he'd lived his life. It was the best guide, but a limited one. Others may go about it according to their own lights. He conveyed his own truths to his daughter, but she'd have to live by her own choices, and the wisdom gained from those choices.

Riley had confidence in her native intelligence. She'd managed better than her father had done. He was optimistic for her. She was an improvement on her struggling parents. They marveled at her quiet, assured manner. Where did it originate?

"I'm going to stop saying how rare it is. I notice that none of my girl friends agree. They hate hearing it. Even Chloe doesn't like it."

"They don't think that true love is rare?"

"They don't want to believe it."

Riley made a face. This was news. The rarity of true love seemed like an axiom to him.

"But maybe they live differently. They just accept what comes along. They meet someone and next thing you know they've moved in with each other, and the battles begin. True love is an empty abstraction. They prefer their own brand, which is completely arbitrary and commonplace. A parade of sloppy relationships."

"It sounds familiar. It reminds me of Jessica. Or Ellie."

"I guess it's rare to want the rare. I think your mother is in fact a rare creature. Maybe I'm one, too. And you must be the same."

He spoke about the things that made Rebecca so unusual. So unlike any other woman he'd ever met. How she knew what people expected of her, but how she was disinclined to conform to their preconceived ideas about her. She took a kind of pleasure in overturning their ungrounded opinions.

Riley had a similar streak. A style of behavior that made him stick out awkwardly in a crowd. At times it even dumbfounded him. He wasn't sure what it was that caused others to pause in silent wonder.

When he was in the army and an officer was walking by, inspecting the troops, he always stopped short in front of Riley. Looking him up and down. Frowning. As if there was something very unacceptable about him. Some obscure quality that upset the officer and made him seethe with indignation. What was it about this odd soldier that made his blood simmer?

When he was a boy he often entertained his friends by playing with words and expressions. He particularly liked questioning cliches that were bantered about.

Their hometown was three hours away from Chicago. The Windy City was the one, exclusive Big City for the Iowans. They always referred to that way. And people always said the same thing. But Riley reversed the trite opinion.

"Chicago is a nice place to live, but I wouldn't want to visit there," he said to his parents.

They immediately caught the joke and laughed. Riley was proud of his clever remark. He liked it when his parents appreciated his wit. But that didn't happen often.

But today his reverse cliche was more than a quip. It was exactly the case when it came to Los Angeles. It wasn't a fun place to visit. It was much better for those who lived in the mystifying city. They were able to understand it from inside, unlike the tourists.

The same must have been true long ago when the boy thought about Chicago. He only saw it from the cornfields over a hundred miles away. It looked so dark and extreme. Very poor and very rich. Happening side by side.

"Can you take a video of me staining the tables," Kristina asked

"Of course. I'll let it run for about a minute and a half and you can edit it down to five or six seconds."

Riley was much better at photographing moving scenes that he was at a single still shot. And Kristina knew how to focus on the brief clip that was most watchable. They realized how to make one thing fascinating and other stuff tediously numbing.

He opened his back door. The tabby was there, raising its head and staring into Riley's eyes. So directly. Then it licked its face, showing the small pointed teeth. It was hungry. He appreciated how silent the cat was. No howling, and mewing, and demanding entrance to the studio. It was like an effective beggar crouching on the side of the road, maybe in a third world country. A powerful will. Playing on Riley's reluctance to seem cold hearted. Without doing anything except sitting at the steel door sphinx-like, an Egyptian statue. Upright, unmoving, focused.

Riley felt manipulated. The way a commandant at a concentration camp could sometimes be forced to change gears by the stares of a group of prisoners. Silence could be like an iron grip around his throat.

Riley had a natural aversion to pets. He liked animals that roamed freely. He didn't want them to feel owned. But some animals weren't buying it. They liked staying close to humans, their distant cousins.

Was Riley this tabby's guardian angel? Or its God? At least its benefactor. A bit heartless, in a way. He didn't observe feeding times. And some days even forgot about it. But the cat's concentrated will power was having its effect.

It reminded Riley of an old fisherman. They would sit for hours drowsing over their pole, waiting for a bite. Riley was like a deep pond which would suddenly cause a strike on the line. And a fish would appear. The cat rushed to the plate and polished it off.

The phone sounded. It was a text from his friend Marjorie. The woman who owned the store in Beverly Hills. She'd recently bought nine paintings. He didn't think he'd hear from her for a long time.

"Hi Riley! How much is this one?"

It was a photo of an extra large colorful painting that he made a month ago.

"Marjorie wants to know how much that big painting is? The one with the L. A. logo. I was going to say $1000."

"A thousand! No way! That's a great piece." Kristina objected.

"But she has to sell it again. I don't know."

"Becauses she bought all those recently?"

"Yes."

"At least $1500."

He wrote back and told her it was $1300. And asked if that would be okay?

"It's fine. It's for a friend of mine. Can she come by and pay you directly? She needs a few more, also."

Kristina was right, once again. Megan wouldn't be selling it again. Even though Riley gave her a low wholesale price.

But, then again, he could make it up on selling the woman a few extra.

Riley always used this method for selling. He kept his eye on the total price. Not the price per unit. This was because he made the art and it didn't cost much to produce it. He could charge whatever he liked, depending on several things. How much money he had in the bank, and how much he presently required. If he was feeling flush he dropped the price and only parted with a few. If he was pinched he dropped the price but pushed for a pile to go out the door.

It was not a good business style, and he was aware of it. But it had gotten him this far, and it was hard to change. He didn't feel right about monkeying with the general pricing structure even when selling to multi-millionaires. A billionaire pays the same as a street bum when it comes to a quart of milk. This was his rationale.

But original paintings by a guy with sixty years experience is different than a quart of milk. At some fundamental level, although he never analyzed what it was. Maybe there were an infinite number of milk quarts, but a very limited supply of Riley O'Kerry paintings.

He liked adding up the projected number of his paintings and dividing them by the number of people in the world. At this point it came out to be around a single painting for around 625,000 human beings living on the earth. That meant one painting for a city the size of Detroit, Memphis, Frankfurt, or Columbo, Sri Lanka. Not to mention dozens in China. Or elsewhere that people never heard of.

Both Warhol and Picasso produced about a half-million works of art because they loved print editions. Riley despised editions. No one wanted his, in any event. He even tried to figure out a way of machine copying his paintings but it always failed. His silkscreens, which were generally used to make editions, simply couldn't do it in his style.

First of all, he couldn't accept visual art on paper. It was too fragile. Too inconvenient. And paradoxically, too expensive. A sheet of a heavy watercolor paper was more expensive than a rough canvas dropcloth, or thin plywood the same size. And then it needed to be framed. Under glass. More cost. Forget about it.

Paper was meant to be used for books. Not paintings. Even Asian calligraphy had to use rather expensive hand-made rice paper. Plus paper required thin ink, or thinned down paint or flaky pastels or charcoal. Not a very lasting medium. All of them.

Painting was delicate enough without going out of your way to make it even more so. It wasn't a chunk of bronze. Or even iron that could rust into nothingness. It didn't have the properties of stone, one of the most durable mediums.

It lay on the stone like a drop of blood. Or an unhappy tear. With a little color added.

Of course the most lasting painting was made from stone. Ground up powdered lapis lazuli or malachite. Mixed with some less durable oil.

If Riley was so concerned about his paintings lasting he'd do well to store them in a pitch black limestone cave deep in the earth. In a country with a lot of desert. Water and light were the enemies of painting. That, and movement from place to place.

He was glad that his studio was always darker than it needed to be. But unfortunately the ceiling had leaks. It didn't rain much in L. A., however. And no painting was ever ruined because of dripping water.

He didn't know whether or not Marjorie was coming to the studio, also. He wrote the address and phone number. Maybe someone would show. It often happened they didn't. Boyle Heights was a walk on the wild side for the Beverly Hills white people. Many found it a step too far. It amused Riley. He never worried about so-to-speak "bad" neighborhoods. He felt right at home in most. In a ritzy neighborhood he would be the one surveilled. He looked out of place, even though he was an old honky. A harmless gavacho.

Riley tidied up the studio, as he always did when a stranger was to arrive. Tidying up meant swabbing bathroom tiled floor, making his bed, and taking out the trash. Not much else.

The joint looked like a somewhat orderly artist's pad. It surprised him when people said it was so neat. What were they expecting? It wasn't neat. Did they see him as a lazy, filthy, hog? Who somehow, by herculean efforts, made himself half-presentable? Almost human. This was probably how he appeared to most.

Face it, he tossed the paint around. More than ever. The spatterings on the floor now reached up to the edge of his bed. The buckets piled up. The tools, also. It would take too

much to ever move. He'd die here. Maybe even Kristina
would, also.

No, she'd have a better fate. Women, even women artists,
weren't as sloppy as their male counterparts. Not even close.
Women liked a comfortable nest. Well-lined with bright
feathers. You couldn't blame them.

It was late in the afternoon. The woman from Beverly Hills
never showed up.

"I think I'm making some headway in my neo-stoicism. If
that's what it is. Say, this lady doesn't come today and buy
the paintings. So what? It certainly isn't going to make me
gnash my teeth and pour ashes over my head."

"Right. It's the same with my men. I'm not losing sleep over
them."

"I'm neither giddy either way. I don't go into ecstasy over a
sale, or despair when it falls through. I refused to be moved
either way."

"But you don't need the money today. Because of the
tenants," Kristina said.

"Right. So I guess stoicism is more than just controlling your feelings. It also means living intelligently and ordering your world as perfectly as possible."

Emotions would be less hectically explosive if a life was lived better, smarter. Feelings are believed to be more powerful than ideas, but they're not always so. As long as the ideas are true and clear. Feelings then can be tamed. If they're not that volcanic.

Robinson Crusoe tamed his wild goats by enclosing them in a pit and denying them food. At a certain point they learned to meekly eat from his hand. This is the way to make our feelings serve us, rather than the reverse.

Riley stopped feeding his childish instincts. It made them more governable.

The phone rang. It was Inga, who hadn't called for almost a month.

"I wanted to thank you for putting the money into my account. Twenty-five dollars, right?"

"Don't mention it."

"It's strange for me. No one ever just handed me money. My family made us earn every penny."

"Well, I don't leave the studio much these days, and never give homeless guys a few dollars every day. So I have to come up with something else."

"I hate to think I'm in that class today. But I have rented a place. It must be about 150 square feet. About $1700 a month. That's what they're charging down here. But it has a kitchen and a bathroom. It's going to hard to paint inside, though."

"So it's not a motel."

"No. It's a unit in a complex. I guess that's what you'd call it. Furnished. And you pay by the week. If we don't have enough for the next week we leave. Sam has a few gigs and I've been scraping off the paint on a house that's going to be repainted. I found an ad for it on craigslist."

"Good for you. But that's hard work. Do you wear a mask?"

"A mask? No, it's too fucking hot for that. Up on a ladder in the sunlight."

"Well, at least it's something to do with painting."

"Didn't quite see it that way. But at least it's some money coming in."

"You're resourceful and work hard. You'll never go down the tubes. You sound good. Not too rattled."

"I'm rattled."

"But you haven't got a gun pressed to your head."

"A gun? Where am I going to get a gun? They're expensive."

"And not about to jump off the ladder and break your neck."

"No, I won't do that. But I still have truck payments, student loan, insurance, telephone and other shit coming at me. How's Kristina?"

"She's fine. Now has a border. A Norwegian kid for a $1000 a month living in a back room. A Lyft driver at night. Doesn't bother her."

"That's good. I saw your latest paintings on Facebook. The ones with the splattered paint. I liked them."

"I'm going to post another one today. It's better than all of them. In my opinion."

Actually Inga sounded better than ever. Maybe sitting around her apartment in West Hollywood for seventeen years was making her exceptionally miserable and obsessive. He recalled how she couldn't sleep and had to jump up and check the locks on her front door a dozen times a night. Hallucinating.

Get a job, baby. He didn't go that far. He wasn't turning into an old fart who dished out shitty advice for anyone anywhere. No. But a paying job, even a brief one or two, wouldn't kill her. And try to stay in that unit, or whatever it was. Week by week.

He'd certainly gone through some rough times. Nor were they conveniently forgotten. They still haunted him. Like the six weeks he was forced to take a construction job in his brother's company. Demolition. Tearing down an old factory building in their hometown. Using a crowbar and hammer. Dirty goddamn work. Covered with dust, dirt, and toxic shit for nearly six weeks.

The only job he ever had after college. No. One more.
Making ornamental iron gates for the Cuban blacksmith. It
lasted about a month. And one more. A part time job at a
gallery in Florida, where he read auction catalogues and
plopped down behind a desk for a few hours.

But other than that, painting and sculpture, and nothing else.
For fifty years. Fifty motherfucking years of anxious toil.
Trying to put food on the table. To even have a table.

How would Inga's life turn out? He wondered about Sam, her
musician husband, who no doubt, was as stunned as she was
about his own present day situation. But, frankly, wasn't it
better than standing around eight hours a day at the music
store on Sunset trying to sell some kid a set of expensive
drums?

If Riley was a musician he rather strum a guitar on a street
corner for a few dollars. Anything but a nine-to-five soul-
exterminating meal ticket.

"No runaway slave has ever starved to death."

Good old Epictetus. It's something to always keep in mind.
Humans are free if they only had the balls to believe it.

They're too steeped in chicken shit to accept their God-given freedom.

We are free to act rather than be acted upon. Always. At every instant. The biggest fight is the daily battle against our passivity.

Our passivity is our inheritance from the inanimate dimension. We have too much calcium, potassium, magnesium, dirt, water, and air in our system. They support life but are not life.

Riley had a sudden access of happiness for his two vagabond friends. They were vagabonds somewhat against their combined wills, but it's working out for them in spite of the fact. What looks like bad luck turns out to be good, and vice versa. They've become active again.

2.

Riley finally finished the Llosa novel. It was a long read. One of those complex books, more like non-literature. In terms of difficulty. Chewiness. Although it's set in a desert town in

Peru it seems like science fiction. The pages are sprinkled with fascinating words that Riley couldn't stop to look up in a dictionary. A Spanish-to-English dictionary, generally.

But it was one of those often tedious reads that made him want to keep plodding on, like a book of philosophy or history. Like a woman who is beautiful but very coy. You are torn between saying goodbye or returning for more.

Riley continued straight through and was rewarded at the end. It was faintly reminiscent of Proust. You wouldn't be able to savor the wonderful irony and humor unless you patiently learned about these characters a page at a time. It was only at the climax that the promised pleasure was fully delivered.

You'd never feel as satisfied if you merely picked up the final chapter and only read that. You wouldn't get the joke. Or feel the strong humanity of the truth about certain people. After reading Llosa's novel Riley now had some more people in his world. Father Garcia, and Bonaficia, were in the same room as Mme. Verdurin and Charlus. These imaginary men and women were as real as actual persons in the world.

But Riley, for all that, began to question the whole meaning of literature. Of inventing, or expressing, stories about this or that human, doing whatever. If he emptied his mind of all the fictional men and women he'd consumed over a lifetime of reading would that be such a tragedy?

Would it leave him deserted and alone, or rather give him more space for the real people that existed and still exist for him?

How is it possible to cleanly separate the two worlds? Famous created characters were more real than people he passed by in the street. But not more real than those who deeply affected him in his ordinary life.

Plus there was another category, one which became more important over time. Those people who Riley read about who were not invented. They were quite real, even if their paths never crossed with his in this world. And, probably, his literary heroes and heroines were always rooted in some real person in the author's life.

Reading expanded his circle. However it was composed. It likely made him consider more carefully the human beings who actually presented themselves to him. They took on an additional weight. Becoming more alive and rounded. Especially if he decided to write about them.

If a painter chooses to portray someone, that person will invariably take on a larger meaning in the painter's life. He will notice insignificant things about them that will make a better, more effective, likeness.

The same is true for a writer who introduces a new character in his writing. But this will always be subject to his personal style. Some people are only a few strokes of a pencil. Others will be captured in stupendous detail. Mona Lisa took three years to complete.

Written characters have the same qualities. The more Riley wrote about this or that person the more alive they became. Less sketchy. More like a full-length traditional oil portrait. But done in a suitably contemporary style.

In some obscure way, people wrote, painted, and sculpted themselves. Riley was just reflecting his mysterious fact. Rebecca was using him as a vehicle for her transmutation into a kind of quasi-immortality. Alchemizing herself. This was also true of Inga, Kristina, Chloe, Knute, Garrick, and so on. Riley was a medium that gave them another aspect. A form of pseudo-deathlessness.

Everything that is, wants to reproduce itself. To be, is to be more. This is true even of inanimate things. Fire wants everything around it to be fire. Snow wants everything that touches it to be cold and wet like itself.

Nothing is satisfied with merely being isolated. Isolation prison cells are the cruelest torture, and defy reality.

"Corrie Ten Boom. What a woman!" Kristina said.

Riley had found the sequel to this person's first book. About her time during WW2 in Holland, and how she, a gentile, helped hide the Jews. Until she was betrayed and picked up by the Gestapo.

The sequel concerns her time in prison and a notorious concentration camp, Ravensbruck. Somehow the name Ravensbruck sounds like a horror novel. It's one of the lesser known camps, but evil enough. The author spent about a half year there and was released before the war ended. Mainly because she wasn't Jewish.

Both father and daughter were amazed by this Dutch woman's courage, as well as her highly unusual Christian faith.

"Just when I want to shove everyone's who's religious into a madhouse I come across this woman. Her incredible belief in

Jesus as the answer to every problem is very odd. It's not how I see things."

"I know. But it works for her." Kristina said.

"And how she sees everything as a possible task to be done for Jesus. Like when she stares at a feeble-minded young girl and decides that she'd open a home for them after the war. Incredible. It's not what goes through my mind when I see a retarded type."

"Mine either. She's different than us. Different than anyone I know."

"You must be born that way. I can't imagine that I could ever become like her, or Mother Teresa."

"I like how she formed a group of other prisoners and they agreed to certain conditions. The first rule was no complaining. I thought, well, I could never be in that group since I complain constantly. And then, no saying negative things about others. But I do that all day long."

"I wonder what they could have talked about? Not much is left for discussion. It seems like it could be a little dull. But actually we spend a lot of time on positive things during our dialogues."

Riley felt that his daughter was too hard on herself. She wasn't like Corrie Ten Boom, nor was she in a concentration camp being tortured and surrounded by murder. Under different circumstances people will respond differently. This was one of the reasons why Riley studied the people who were forced into an extreme environment. He supposed he could learn some lessons about what he might do if it ever came to that.

"Funny how Raphael doesn't like acting," he said, referring to his grandson.

"No. He doesn't."

"But he's a natural for that."

"But maybe it's best that he doesn't start too early."

"Right. Child actors often have trouble later in life. He's handsome enough and has the easiest time memorizing lines. Plus he isn't the least bit shy. But he's exceptionally unmoved by anything that he doesn't immediately love."

"He simply won't do something because someone else wants him to. He's outraged if anyone tries to force him. What he doesn't love he hates. Or what he doesn't love doesn't exist."

"He reminds me a bit of you, and just about everyone he's related to. His dad, Rebecca, Rainer's dad and mom. Even me. But he's a pure version of all of us. He's totally himself. I was much too influenced, and bent every which way by other people."

Riley's grandson comes from a long line of intransigent types. Stubborn as a team of mules. Non-conforming. Rebellious.

He hoped he could live long enough to see how the grand opera ends, or at least until the plot begins to truly unfold.

Raphael wanted his grandfather to make a graphic novel.

"You'd be good at it!" the boy said. He'd just bought one from the comic book store.

"I once thought I would," Riley mused. "I loved cartoons when I was young. I made some digital ones a few years ago and my brothers got the biggest kick out of them. But they took a long time. I spent way too long on a frame. I never could complete an actual strip."

"You should try!"

But Riley was as stubborn as his grandson. He was busy enough with his paintings and non-graphic novels. How much more could he be expected to create? The idea, however, had charm. Maybe in another life.

Riley began painting, and Kristina stained her table tops.

"I discussed humor the other day with Raphael. He loves this one actor. Jonah Hill."

"He's funny."

"Right. He is. And Raphy showed me this clip of him and an actress. I said Jonah was funny but the girl wasn't. She was beautiful, but not funny. He was puzzled. Then I explained some of the differences between those who can make you laugh, and those who can't. We talked about people we know. He said 'daddy's funny.' I couldn't let it slide. No, honey, daddy's not funny. Raphy was surprised to hear it. Daddy's very handsome and serious. But he can't make people laugh. Raphael went away thinking about it."

"Right. Being funny-looking helps a person to be funny. I've said it a hundred times. Marilyn Monroe doesn't crack anyone up. Beauty and humor don't mix very well."

"I wonder if Inga would agree. She's funny, but wouldn't like to be thought funny looking."

"Yes, but she knows she isn't a pro. She's not stand-up comedian. I use to beg her to try out an open mike, but she refused. I said just drink a quart of vodka and go on stage and shoot your mouth off. She didn't like the idea. I hope Raphael doesn't feel that way about acting."

"And she's odd about her looks, too."

"She's kind of a blend of comical and attractive. Not too much of either. Or just enough, I guess. She'll say 'I am absolutely GORGEOUS!' But I don't think she believes it."

They switched back to books. Riley wanted to say something about the Gorky he was reading. The third part of a trilogy of Russia's favorite Soviet author. Kristina didn't care much for this one. Too political for her. She loves novels about love, but politics leaves her cold. Riley didn't feel the same way.

"The remark I liked most from last night was where some character, an old man, said to the young seeker that the only thing we should be angry about is our own rotten life. This was clear enough for me. Not life in general, or the rulers like the czar, or bosses, teachers, cops, and other authorities, but we need to direct our anger at our willingness to lead downtrodden, rotten lives."

"That's true. I feel that way about myself at times. Especially when I'm angry at Rainer."

"Our anger is almost perpetually misplaced. Our finger needs to point back at its source. Our own stupidity and cowardice."

"I notice that Michael Baker is always complaining about how women have exploited him and made him suffer. He doesn't realize it was his own choice to start with them in the first place. He's the type of man who always goes for the hot babe who ends up treating him like shit."

"Men are such dimwits. Women, too. They go nuts over some hunk and he dumps on their head and they scream like it's the end of the world. What did they expect? Lower their aim."

"If people made more appropriate choices they wouldn't have so much to whine about."

"But a lot of them don't want to do that. And so the wailing and sobbing goes on and on. Not to mention the occasional homicide."

"When I go to dinner with Michael Baker tonight I'll have to be more upfront with him. Here. Look at this picture."

She showed her dad a photo of a man's face. He had dark rings around his eyes and sharp angles at his jawline and cheekbones. A pale, gaunt man. Not well, perhaps.

"You've mentioned his eating phobias. He looks like he's trying out for a part in a film about Dachau."

"I said he is way too thin."

"It's more than that. Only about one out of ten anorexics are men, so it's very unusual. He might have some condition. But he's probably into some strict diet. Reducing his calories to zero in order to extend his life. It's a strategy that's been around for awhile."

"No calories. RIght. He wouldn't nibble at my desert the other night. Not a crumb. And vitamins, too. Bottles of them."

"He imagines he's going to live to 150, or maybe longer. But what a life! Why would it be even worth it to starve yourself like that. It isn't the length of years that matter most, but how much we enjoy the ones we have."

Riley thought that a brief thrilling life was better than a long tortured one, if it came to that. Long versus short was a subject he examined again and again. While it was true that he already had lived an acceptable number of years he'd like to experience a few more if possible. He still had rows to hoe.

"And here's another thing to consider about this radical concept. If reduction of caloric intake is the road to an extra long life why aren't people in Africa and India, say, outliving the flabby creatures in America? Look at the differing statistics on mortality rates in the two cultures. But I'm sure he'll have a ready answer to this."

"I'll bring it up to him."

"I don't think you'll make a dent."

When a person wanders down the wrong path it gets harder with every step until he's unable to take another. It's only at that point when he turns around and changes direction. Whether or not this man has reached his limit is impossible to tell. He alone knows how much he can endure. He will come to that conclusion when it's time.

Riley reflected on this common plight. Everyone goes through something like it over a lifetime. We all have our breaking point. Riley, at one time, considered a philosophy that would describe such a process. He even had a name for the crisis. A term he borrowed from a German mystic: the fiery punctum.

A punctum was Latin for point. It was a painful point in a person's development. A burning, unendurable, hellish point. This excruciating point was the psychological barrier that no one could pass. The necessary pain was on a scale that went from a mild pin prick up to an insane degree of blazing fury.

In other words, it was a daily occurence. Something in every rational brain that said yes or no. This highly adjustable inner function was the source of universal right and wrong.

In some people there was an even, clear flow between their feelings and this inner guide. In others it was weak and murky. Why this was so was a complicated issue.

The end points on this guiding spectrum were either painful or pleasurable. The man Kristina was describing was heading toward the dark end of the navigational setup, and the signs were there for anyone to see. But a person was also able to head toward the bright punctum. The radiant end-point of sweetness and fulfillment.

Riley received a text. It read:

"I have a Riley O'Kerry painting. A Brigitte Bardot that is falling apart and I would love to have it repaired."

It was followed by a name and a phone number. The artist was bound to receive notes like this, and the only surprise was that he didn't receive more of them. Paintings were fragile, no matter how they were constructed. Riley had spent most of his time figuring out how to make them stronger and less prone to damage. But he still had a long way to go.

A Bardot painting could be over twenty years old, and visibly almost ruined. At that time Riley just painted and sold them as quickly as he could without worrying too much about how they'd be able to ward off the accidents of time and space.

When his paintings started to really sell that speeded up the process, but also revealed how vulnerable they were. Almost immediately problems arose. People tore the canvas, spattered and marred it, punched it from behind, etc. He was like a doctor on an emergency call to a number of homes.

The better the work became the more it was able to resist the assaults of time. In fact, this toughening up of his painting almost became the deciding factor. He recalled when he drove across Florida to drop off a canvas and by the time he got there the painting was already scratched and scuffed up. It couldn't be sold in that condition. It forced Riley to take these problems with the utmost seriousness.

After that, he kept one eye always on this aspect. How would a painting look after moving around among careless types after a number of years. You couldn't count on their sensitivity, or delicate handling.

It was likely to pass through a crowd of ignorant louts. That was its fate. The destiny it shared with humanity's greatest treasures as well as their worthless garbage. Don't kid yourself, Riley. People will not give your paintings as much respect as you'd wish for. Prepare them for this journey.

He was now at that stage as a painter where his style was little more than an attempt to armor plate his work, making it as bullet proof as possible. He was aware of all the astonishing variety of mistreatment his work was subject to. He knew his enemy by now. He was ready for the next battle.

3.

Another morning, How many does he have left? What about the next life? Would there be mornings in that world? Would it have a sun and a turning planet full of former earthlings? Or would it be flat and stationary? Or maybe have two suns, one fainter, which would resemble a kind of overcast night. Riley thought this was a possibility.

He stumbled into the bathroom. Passing by the dead rat that he knew was laying there. He'd been awakened by the sound of the trap springing shut, catching the pest on its nose. Two nights earlier he'd heard the bottle of cooking oil tumble over. Those things don't just happen without a cause. He survey the spilled oil on the kitchen table. No, something had pushed the bottle over on its side. It was too heavy for a mouse or cockroach. And no racoons had ever been spotted inside the studio. All the cats were outside in the alley. Ergo, a rat.

Well, one less nuisance in the world, he said as he carried it to the trash container and dropped it in. A black cat watched him as he tossed the trap with the dangling rat inside and shut the top. Why weren't you doing your job? He asked the green-eyed cat. Who looked a little guilty. Or was displaying its normally inscrutable poker face.

But perhaps the cats were letting Riley know that they needed to be inside the studio if he expected them to be on the nightly prowl. No, they will remain outside. He'll deal with the occasional rat.

Okay then, suit yourself. The black cat walked away.

He wondered if there were any people left with a last name of Ratcatcher. Like Emily Ratcatcher. Or Josiah Ratcatcher. He was sure that there was such a surname like that somewhere, left over from the middle ages. Like Baker, Cooper, Smith, Carpenter, and so on. Family names derived from their way of making a living.

If there was such a family today the name was probably abbreviated into something more socially acceptable. Like

Ratcher. Rachitt. Reacher. Raker. Until it was hidden from its original profession.

He'd went outside this morning because he was out of coffee. He'd been out for two days. Yesterday he merely ran some hot water over the used grounds and been content with a very thin cup or two. But by today that wouldn't have worked.

He drove up Whittier to Vallarta, one of the two supermarkets he used. The morning couldn't be better, as far as the weather went. Mild, golden haze. People on their way to work. A long line of cars heading toward downtown. Women doing their grocery shopping already.

A dark-skinned man shuffled toward the entrance to the supermarket. He was wearing layers of soiled blankets, resembling a medieval monk. A mendicant? But Riley watched him stop at the deli counter and even pull out a bill of some kind.

They were out of his usual brand of coffee and he had to pay extra for another can. He then bought a banana muffin to complete his breakfast.

He stopped at a gas station on the way back to the studio, and pumped twenty dollars worth into the pickup. He was behind a young black man who was driving a much fancier car than the old painter. Riley watched as the black guy carefully washed and wiped the windows to his newer model Nissan.

The water boiled and Riley poured it over the fresh espresso grounds. He was feeling more optimistic as he sat down and logged on.

He noticed a few new books were being published. One by a celebrity woman that catalogued her struggles with booze. Another was a diary of a woman who was murdered in the Holocaust and the handwritten manuscript had sat hidden in a bank vault for seventy years.

It's been suggested that each person has at least one book inside of them. That seems to be true. Anyone who'd lived at least thirteen years on earth could probably describe his or her life in around one hundred pages.

But this wasn't done. Or only by a precious few. Why? Riley theorized that people weren't very proud of their existence. Didn't treat it with that much consideration. Didn't really feel the need to put it down in black and white. Who would conceivably care about me? That must be what goes through many minds.

What would be the answer to that question? Well, maybe not many might care that much about you. But a few, or at least one other person. Everyone has someone who would be interested enough to read about them.

Riley recalled the time a woman asked him what he did at night.

"I'm writing my autobiography," he said.

She laughed. And said "But, Riley, you haven't done . . . I mean . . . who would . . . "

She tried to be as polite as she could be, but wasn't able to complete the sentences.

This took place when Riley had just turned forty. He didn't need this woman to tell him that he'd never done anything worth sharing with a far wider audience. He was more acutely aware of it than she could ever be.

This woman, a somewhat educated type, must have thought only great, deeply admired, worthy human beings deserve to have a book about themselves. Even written by themselves.

Who the fuck did he think he is? Talk about absurd. I mean .
. .

But if you asked her who deserves to have a book published
about them you might have laughed at the people she would
have suggested. She may have been stumped for a second,
but then would have mentioned a few people whose name is
already forgotten.

People are historically great because they're written down,
and not the other way around. Not everyone understands
this.

Riley realized that he had to write himself down. Like any
human he was worth a single autobiography. It's just that this
single book had many individual volumes that comprised one
enormous tome taking up a seven foot long bookshelf.

 It will require one hundred separate volumes to complete the
book of Riley's stay on earth. His bible.

This newly published diary by the Holocaust victim ended the
day she was murdered. But so far no one has murdered
Riley. His story therefore goes on.

He called the man who owned the damaged Bardot painting.

"Grant Busby, please," Riley said in a grave tone.

"Yesss."

"This is Riley O'Kerry."

Silence.

"You wrote me about a Brigitte Bardot painting."

"OH! Yes! Oh, thank you for answering my email. It's you! I'm so happy to talk to you!"

"Okay."

"I've had your painting for over twenty years. And I LOVE it! But it's falling to pieces. The gesso is crumbling. And I don't know what to do. I now have it stored. A friend saw it yesterday and asked why is this here? In the garage! I said I looked all over for you but couldn't find you. He said he'd try. Did he contact you yet?"

"No."

"Oh, this is great that I have you on the phone. I'm driving on the 405, and it's madness. As usual. I bought the Brigitte at a charity auction. I think I paid $2300 for it. And I used to hang it in the properties that I have listed. I'm a realtor. But before that I taught at Cal Arts. Graphic design. For years. I own a collection of contemporary art. Kenny Sharf, Sam Francis, and many others. But I love the Brigitte. It was hanging in a condo I sold to Meryl Streep. She loved it. And she's married to an artist, Don Gummer. He loved it, too."

"Really? Great."

Riley let the man talk. He was entertaining. An older gay guy. And stuck in traffic.

"I also was a Vogue photographer for years. I know so many artists. I can introduce you to Ed Ruscha. Your work reminds me of a cross between a Ruscha and Pop art. It's so fresh. Do you really think you could fix my Brigitte?"

"I can fix anything that I've made. And it wouldn't be the first time. So, you weren't the original owner. People are careless with their paintings. With all their art. But I can make it look good again. Where is the damage? Is it on the image?"

"The image?"

"Yes. The image. On Brigitte. Or is it on the background. She's no doubt surrounded by another color."

"It's on both! I love her, too. She's never had anything done to her face. And she's an animal rights activist."

"Yes. A genuine film goddess. There are only a few."

"I have a friend that you must meet. She's so beautiful and she's an actress and deserves to be in that category. Julie Newmar."

"Right. I've thought about painting her but never have."

"Oh, you should! She's 85 today. And still ravishing! Six foot four! I always take her as my date to these charity functions."

Riley had an image of Julie Newmar in some sort of catwoman costume. He hadn't heard anything about her recently, except for some brawls with one of her neighbors.

"Sam Francis used to go crazy when he saw her."

"Yeah, I can see that."

Riley had a picture in his head of the late painter of colorful abstractions. He liked the art. That is, the technique used. The man's work was instantly recognizable as belonging to him and no one else. Something that had up to now eluded him. Even though people would often say they could tell an O'Kerry from far away.

"But what should I do next? I'll pay you for the work you do on my Brigitte. This is so exciting."

"Do you have a pickup?"

"A pickup? No. I can rent a truck, but it'll have to be covered. And carefully placed inside. I live in Brentwood."

Riley was almost going to suggest just tossing it in the back of a pickup, but he realized that wouldn't have sounded good.

He opened up a bit with the man on the phone, who wanted to chat, for a variety of reasons. Riley was finished with his painting and writing for the day, and was sitting comfortably in his chair, staring at his latest work. He told him a few things about his art, but he had to frequently interrupt the flow coming from the collector, who was so informed about the local art scene. Something Riley had ignored, and was ignored by.

But it no longer was that important to him. He didn't need the sales. He was starting to paint in what might become his signature style.

The other guy rattled on.

"Then there was the time I had to take some photos of Ellsworth Kelly. God, what a sulky bore. He didn't say a word. Just sat there, wishing it was over, and I'd get the fuck out of his life."

"Painters are weird. It's how they are. But you'd think Kelly, being Irish, or at any rate having an Irish last name, would be a little more talkative."

Riley had little good to say about other painters. As far as their intelligence goes. They often seemed not very intellectual. Certainly not well read. As dumb as musicians. No better. Neither had to be able to read and write. And it showed.

Talented illiterates for the most part. At least today's bunch. To be able to paint or play an instrument didn't require anything special in the way of brain power. No DaVinci in today's art world. Not even close. Riley had a hard time believing that Warhol was anything more than a half-wit. And he greatly admired Warhol. For his creative ambition.

But Riley only knew a few artists. They weren't the basis for his friendships. He wasn't drawn to them any more than anyone else he'd meet. He recalled Pollock saying that friendship was overrated. He was compelled to agree. When a man was wholly driven to paint a friend was only in the way.

"The art world. A person needs someone to sponsor him. Kenny Sharf was lost until he found that one sponsor. After that it was beautiful for him. This is the way it is for all of them. It's not that one is so much more than the others. It's just that he has someone to back him. Oh, I know them all! And I love your work."

He then bewailed the high prices of contemporary art. The man must have a setup that allows him to gab on the freeway. He was fine, just yakking away. Riley broke in when he felt like it.

"Well, one thing I can say about myself. I've democratized my painting. I've put thousands of pieces into the hands of thousands of ordinary people. Not millionaires, but them, too."

Later on he sent a picture of the Bardot. It had several white blotches where the paint fell off, or was knocked off. It was an early painting where Riley had experimented with various kinds of plaster. On top of different textiles. Maybe not a good marriage between the two. He'd be able to make it presentable. It'd be different, though.

The man would bring it to the studio in a few days. The more Riley thought about it the more he actually liked the way it looked just as it is. It resembled a fresco from an ancient ruin. Like the ones dug up at Pompeii. Missing parts tended to add to the appeal, as far as the artist was concerned. It was a style in itself.

But he'd fill them in anyway. Because he was the original painter, and still able to do so. He'd also keep his insights available for the future. Maybe they'd point the way to a new style.

"They're on their way to pick up the tables," Kristina said. The large order for Michael Baker was done, and about to be delivered to his new business down in Orange County.

She'd worked particularly hard on them, and the wood gleamed. They were custom pieces, long and narrow. Over twelve feet by less than three foot. Riley saw them as

potentially tipsy. But they could always be bolted to the floor.
He thought that would be mandatory. But the customer
insisted on those proportions, probably because of spatial
necessity.

"Here's a picture of his new place. He doesn't have good
taste. Look at those signs."

Riley examined the half-finished location. It didn't have that
much going for it. But it was going to a large restaurant.

"I have a feeling that this project will not end abruptly."

"No. He calls me about six times a day. I guess I'm getting to
see it from both sides now."

Riley was surprised it had taken so many years for his
daughter to find herself on the receiving end of a person's
passionate desire. It was probably due to her established role
as an active lover rather than a passive beloved. She refused
to become the object of a man's obsessive curiosity.

Human desire was a very unequal business. Everyone had
their designated place in a drama. But it wasn't unusual to try
out a new role, just to see how it felt. Like a musician picking

up a trumpet instead of playing a piano. Or a lawyer opening up a coffee shop. Just for extra knowledge.

Kristina only spent time with men she was clearly attracted to. Michael Baker was a novelty. A big switch for her. And not one to be repeated any time soon.

"I think I'll go back to Gerard."

Gerard was her first man. Before this French film actor she was a virgin. Riley recalled the night his daughter called him from the hotel room. "Dad, I just had sex!" He was aware that it wasn't very common for daughters to immediately phone their fathers after such an event. But neither was he the only man in history that had ever taken such a call.

But they always had an open-hearted, easy going relationship. It seemed to come naturally to them.

"The other day he called me after his work was finished. He wanted to drive two hours in the worst kind of rush hour traffic to take me out for sushi that night. All for a little peck of kiss. I couldn't believe it."

"Now you have evidence that men are ruled by desire. They'll do anything for a little taste of honey. If it's the particular honey they dream of."

"I would never have believed it until it's right in front of me."

"And by way of contrast you can now judge of those men who aren't that overwhelmed by passion for you. No matter what they say."

"Exactly. Eric wouldn't even drive two blocks to see me. Are all men this way?"

"I don't know. I only know what I've experienced. Eva would call me up and ask me to come and see her even if it was only for a half hour. I'd drive for an hour each way. All for nothing. Not even a kiss on the cheek. Men can lose their minds over a woman. And women can do the same over a man."

"I certainly realize that. But Eva must have wanted to see you more than I want to see Michael Baker."

"That's true. I don't think I was as repulsive in her eyes as he is in yours. But somehow she never has gone crazy over a man. Even her husbands and boyfriends."

"Because she's more ambitious. She doesn't let herself get swept away."

"It sounds odd to us. We let ourselves become overwhelmed by desire. But not everyone is like us. Eva is more overwhelmed by luxuries. By wealth. And feelings of achievement. Her own dreams demand fulfillment. And they aren't dreams of men. Men are simply stepping stones. She's as ambitious as an ambitious man."

"Not like Rebecca, certainly."

"No. Your mother is a passionate lover. She never took her other accomplishments that seriously. Her focus was on men, and the need to find one that wholly validated her existence. And she's much better at pushing men forward, rather than pushing herself."

Riley wondered if he was describing Rebecca's daughters in the same breath. Each of them loved men, but not as intensely as their mother did. Davi was married to an Israeli and with four sons. Chloe had a few major lovers, but was dedicated to her writing as well. Kristina had only the smallest number of men in her life. She really had a highly focused view of them. Either they were what she wanted, or they didn't break the surface.

The daughters resemble their mother to varying degrees. But all were distinctly individualized. Maybe because they came from different fathers. Whatever the case the entire family was more like a cut and pasted collage than a seamless unity. This had a definite charm in Riley's eyes. He felt this was his family more than any family that ever existed for him. Other families never held much interest for him. Even his Midwestern Catholic family always made him feel a little too alien. He had more in common with Jewish gang. The sense of belonging was actually stronger.

Kristina was influenced by a short essay by Pascal. Her father had brought it to her attention. Even though he hadn't read it in nearly fifty years. It was in a textbook and he had his students read it. For the year where he taught literature at a military junior college in Missouri. So long ago. Amazing that it stayed with him. Pascal's essay. Which apparently was only attributed to him.

It was late Saturday night and he found it again online. He read it over carefully and was stunned to see how it must have affected the rest of his adult life. The ideas he held today were nearly all traced to that powerfully insightful essay on love. He wondered how it even had managed to be inserted into a textbook.

"Love and ambition don't go together," Kristina reported.

Pascal said both are important and even essential for a complete human life. But they tend to annul each other if they occupy the same heart and mind simultaneously. And it's best to begin with love and end with ambition.

Pascal died young. At 39. But if anyone was a child genius when it came to philosophy it was him. How could he have seen such truths from such a young perspective?

The idea that ambition, best suited to a person who has already gone beyond passionate desires for another person, is an insight that might make sense to someone who has reached age sixty. Not a young man barely thirty. What can he possibly know for sure?

It's probably for this reason that the essay is only attributed to him. Although Riley couldn't find any detailed information about it online. Whoever wrote it knew something profound about the subject. Pascal might have been a virgin. Odd.

Ambitious men or women never stop being ambitious. You can say that people stop feeling amorous over the years. But ambition doesn't have any physical checks. It can go on until the grave. And even further.

Riley saw it as a kind of lunacy. But, on the other hand, he was an example of it, too. Wasn't he increasingly devoted to his personal quest? To become a great painter, and even a great writer? Don't laugh. Ambition isn't hindered by mere snickering. Mockery may defeat lesser passions, but not undiluted, expansive ambition.

There are plenty of examples to choose from. Whether living or dead. And it's easy to see that gargantuan ambition utterly slams the door on any residue of former love. Physical desires for sex are once and for all eliminated as if they never were in the first place.

"I simply can't imagine any woman, anywhere, no matter how sublimely beautiful she is, standing between me and painting," Riley announced to his daughter. And he kept returning to this fact.

He was dumbfounded by the changes in himself. They began slowly but ruthlessly and ceaselessly advanced like a marauding army. But by now he was a new old man. And very adamant about it.

"I received a text from Philippe this morning," Kristina said.

She showed it to Riley.

"Just ordered your father's book. I am currently in Berlin but it should be there when I get back home."

"What the fuck! For some reason this disturbs me," he said. "You told me that Philippe hates to think of himself as a character in a book. I'm not sure why, but apparently so. And he must thumb through the pages, hunting for his nom de plume."

"Probably. You said you've sold some novels in England, right?"

"Yes. No doubt one arrived at his address. It bothers me to think that people want to see how they're portrayed. It's like someone looking over my shoulder as I write. It cramps my style. I'm glad that Inga or Aylish or Rainer don't read. I can breathe easier and write more sincerely. Otherwise I feel censored. Not pleasant."

Riley went back and reread any passages in the last novel where the name Philippe came up. He was a little puzzled to see how nicely he was treated by Kristina. She said some flattering things about the man. Mainly by way of comparison. Philippe's successors fell quite short of the raffish European.

Kristina mostly involved herself with American males and Riley felt sympathy for her.

"What do Frenchwomen think of American men?" Riley once asked Marcel, his bi-cultural friend.

"Not much. They find them very boring."

Riley could understand. He'd been with a few French-Canadians from Montreal and they seemed to run circles around him. He wasn't sure exactly why. But he did his best to somehow improve. Less of a Yankee oaf. Maybe he was a little better today. But difficult to judge.

"Did you ever hear about the tables that were delivered?" Riley asked his daughter.

"I did. He wrote and said they are superb. He loves the heavy iron legs and the tops. How you can see the grain, and the irregularities."

"Good. He might have had a different response."

"I'm proud of him. He didn't act like an idiot. He hasn't even called me."

"That's to his credit."

"And he knows it's my birthday in a few days. He says he has this present for me. He already gave me one. A ridiculous charger for my phone that doesn't even work. But he kept saying how he has a bigger present. As if he's trying to tempt me into going out with him one more time."

"Seems very immature."

"I know. He can't become natural around me. Everything is jarring. He's jumpy and all elbows. Everything is off. As if he's on drugs. I'll bet he is. Always late, and having to go on a pointless errand."

"I just thought of another explanation. Maybe he only worried about you completing the job. Making sure his ten grand was safe."

"That's a funny idea. He was dating me to keep a close eye on his tables."

"Right. Now that the project is finished he can vanish."

"He was very odd about money. When I told him how much Rainer gives me each month he was flabbergasted."

"At how little it is?"

"No, how much it is! He doesn't give this women any money for his child. And he keeps complaining over and over about how his own mother is suing him."

"But you said he never even lived with this woman. How can he be sure it's his child?"

"He probably isn't. I saw a photograph and didn't see much of him in the girl."

"He must like to think of her as his. As long as he isn't paying anything to raise her. If the woman wants support then he might ask for a DNA test."

"But I was proud of him that he didn't offer any bogus criticisms of the tables. And maybe we've seen the last of Michael Baker. I just got a call about another order from this high tech company in Santa Monica."

They're moving forward once again. People appear, corral their time and energy, then vanish. At least for awhile. Maybe forever.

Riley had a flashing insight as he lay in his claw-footed, enameled cast iron bathtub. It felt like another step closer to the ultimate gathering fusion. Where his painting, writing, sculpting, emotions, and thoughts all attained an unprecedented oneness.

Along with this realization came another passing notion. The Point Omega. He hadn't thought about Teilhard de Chardin in many years. He read the Jesuit priest's main book in college, where it was taught in a course of some kind. He couldn't recall the name.

It was another example of how his early studies must have unconsciously survived and even steered him in his future explorations.

Why would it be so hard to believe that the present is the outcome of previous choices?

Not only that, but the present also conditions the lure of the future.

Riley took a particular path because of a subtle hint of things to come. Just as an animal sniffs the air and moves in the direction of its next meal. The future wafts toward us as a promise of fulfillment. We're willing to go through all kinds of hell to get there.

So about this Omega Point. This end point. What was it anyway? He remembered meeting the husband of one of Rebecca's childhood friends. This man had devised through the study of Latin American anthropology that the world was on the verge of a stunning "harmonic convergence." A kind of end of the world prophecy, from an Aztec angle.

But it never exactly happened. And then he died. Riley could still see him as he went for his morning hike, carrying his flute. Gentle, aloof, composed. But maybe the harmonic convergence somehow, in some personal sense, did come true for him. But for no one else.

And now Riley was also experiencing something similar. A type of collectedness, like fingers interlacing. Or where threads were weaving together into a coherent pattern.

He planned on making a different kind of painting this week. Not radically different, but different enough. It would be a return to his word art. But not as romantically based. Nor even as philosophical.

Riley understood how some of his texts were a little too learned. Latin phrases, clever twists, obscure words. And people found them hard to grasp. As if they might be a private witticism, or something too ironic for widespread consumption.

No one wants to be laughed at. No one would dare to buy a painting if they felt the secret joke was on them.

There was an old idea that art is actually a way to conceal art.

Instead of aiming to show how brilliant he is, Riley would be better off keeping all that to himself.

The new paintings would simply take a passage from his novels. Nothing that astounding. Any sentence might do. Mysteries in broad daylight. That sort of thing.

And he'd no longer use a silkscreen for the words. He'd paint them in his own hand. You couldn't call it calligraphy. Riley had a very untrained handwriting. But it was his own, at least. And he had finally figured out a technique for conveying this. By using the edge of a small roller he was able to create a linear effect. Like a pen, or brush. But it had a novel look to it. Crude, but real.

To counterbalance the childish barbarism of his long hand script he could always use a
technically sophisticated silkscreened design somewhere on the side of the painting. It would then be a combination of mechanical and personal. This would qualify it for a successful contemporary, even avant garde, painting.

He already had a phrase in mind. Not something lifted from his writing. Just an everyday comment. But it had a connotative value. It resonated into several distinct areas.

"I think I'll make a painting and then scrawl these words on it," he said to Kristina. "What about the body."

"What about the body?"

"Yes."

Kristina seemed nonplussed. Neither enthusiastic, nor unimpressed. Waiting for a further explanation.

"It's one of those remarks that could refer to a number of things. To me it sounds like two men plotting a murder. What would they do with the corpse? Or maybe it's a couple of metaphysicians discussing their system. What part does the body play in their vision. Or it could be two friends evaluating a third person. As a potential mate or lover. It also reminds me of Nazis trying to figure out how to cover their tracks in their genocidal goals. Bodies are a problem. How to safely dispose of them. And so on."

"All right." Still unconvinced, perhaps.

"But whenever I think about the next painting I realize that it's a mistake to plan it out too thoroughly beforehand. It never ends up that way. Something is always discovered in the act of making it. Otherwise it'd merely be a crafted object, like an omelet or a rocking chair."

"And not something creative?"

"Right. If you already knew what it was going to be before you actually made it that would detract from its artistic category. A teapot will be teapot even before the potter begins to touch the clay. This isn't true of an artful painting."

"You don't know where it'll end up?"

"Exactly. It only has to be itself. And serve no other function."

Riley could talk about this subject endlessly. A painting is an object that causes the viewer to intensely dream. To repeatedly dream over. To question existence in a new way.

Something to challenge a person's poorly grounded beliefs. In a pleasurable manner. To bring about a kind of harmless crisis in their thinking. Causing a delicate opening in their lives. Like reading a love letter from an intriguing stranger.

Painting is like a rock jutting out of a flowing river. Something durable, stationary, opposed to transience. An eternal reality in spite of circumstances and temporal changes.

They were at their neighborhood thrift store and Kristina walked up to him, holding a long playing vinyl record.

"Does it make sense to buy this for only one song?"

It was an album by Kim Carnes, and her one hit wonder. Betty Davis Eyes.

"It's a pretty catchy tune."

"And it's what Chloe wants to be played at her funeral."

Riley didn't know that. Chloe did actually resemble a young
Bette Davis, with her hooded eyes. People now and then
mentioned it, but not as much lately. Maybe Bette Davis was
starting to fade from popular view.

"What song do you want played at yours?"

"Angel Baby."

It's somewhat of a lullaby from the 1950's that Rebecca used
to sing to Kristina when she was a baby. Her little face used
to light up. She still likes hearing it.

So much music from 1950 to 1980, or thereabouts, was on
the rather gentle side. A lot of cooing and mewing. Sweetly
affectionate. They're still being produced and sung, but not as
frequently. Times change, and the songs with them.

"I don't want a funeral, or anything remotely like it," Riley said,
"but to be cremated, and have my ashes dumped on the 10
freeway. Still, if there were to be a funeral I'd like them to play
'Red, Red Wine" by UB40. I looked up that video last night
and it still is great. And somehow reminds me of my younger
self."

The black and white video showed a British kid getting drunk at a pub and having his money stolen from him. It was skillfully created. A gem of a small story. And it did recall his early days of carousing and recklessness.

Today he only drank wine at his meals in the studio. And no more than a half-bottle. But it was an improvement on his college days. He loved the reggae beat of the red wine song, although he never paid close attention to the words. They just didn't matter. Like the words in any good popular tune. He enjoyed the refrain, whatever it supposedly meant.

"I think I'll ask some more people about what tune they'd want to hear. Not that a corpse would hear anything."

"Jessica would like 'Celebration!' So her."

"Celebration? I don't even know who sings it."

"Kool and the Gang."

"Okay. Hm. But it does seem to capture her spirit. Inga would like to hear 'Pretty Woman'".

"A good choice."

"I think she'd even expect people to pick that out for her. I wonder what your mom would choose? I think I'll ask her."

He texted Rebecca later on that night. He was concerned that she might take it the wrong way, whatever that might mean. As if we were sitting around imagining her death. But, no, she got the idea, and wrote back the following morning.

"I think the part of Mozart's concerto piano, andante from Elvira Madigan. Or 'My Girl' (but that sounds like a Davi choice). The whole concerto is too long."

Davi is Rebecca's first daughter, currently living in Israel.

Riley thought she might pick something classical. It was more Jewish to do so. Like Professor Manny, who didn't even know anything musically un-classical.

He couldn't remember if he saw Elvira Madigan with Rebecca, or with his wife, Sara. But he also loved the score in that film.

Yet he wrote her back.

"Interesting. Have to ask Oliver about his preferred music. Could you choose a tune we could all remember and hum now and then? But it's your funeral, as they say."

She wrote back:

"Oh, I will think about it. Maybe "Satisfaction" by the Stones, or "Love Me Tender" by Elvis. It sounds even better."

Then later on: "Hey Jude."

It was not easy to get people to play along with them. Kristina, Chloe, and Riley were aware of this difficulty. They were always prepared for a negative reply when they asked something of anyone.

"It's better to ask things of yourself, but only once in awhile of other people. I notice my brother George asks questions on social media. Always questions which he could simply answer without even taking any trouble."

"He does? Why do you think he does that?" Kristina wondered.

"Because he wants some connection with a person. Remember when Vera used to write these long hand letters to us and they were always filled with questions? She just wanted us to answer. To keep in touch. But it's a little pathetic."

Then Rebecca mentioned Riley's will. Did he have it all taken care of? Making sure to leave Kristina the building. And, in the horrible event of her dying before her son, adding a clause so that the property ended up with his grandson. In trust, until he reaches thirty.

Rebecca comes from a family of lawyers. People who concern themselves with wills and those sort of things. Riley had one brother who also was a retired lawyer. And Rebecca was living with Oliver, one more of the same tribe. They came in handy.

Riley recalled that he was enrolled in "pre-law" as an undergraduate. You had to choose something. But he never dreamed of becoming a lawyer. Mainly because this was the conclusion of a psychological test he had administered to him as a teen. It said he was better suited for law than art. This infuriated him. And made slighted annoyed with lawyers ever since.

Picasso refused to draw up a will. He wouldn't let anyone speak of death in his presence. He must have been superstitious, and of course it led to huge problems after he finally died.

But Riley had nothing to leave anyone, at least in comparison with rich artists. His old brick studio was worth something. And that was it. Except for a collection of his paintings that may or may not have value.

And there was the matter of carving up his little domain. What sort of inheritance could he leave his stepdaughters, Chloe and Davi? He felt close to both, without really seeing them that often. It had been decades since he saw Davi. But time didn't make much difference in these things. Chloe, on the other hand, lived in L. A.

Originally he planned on leaving a percentage of his estate ("estate" What a joke!) to the daughters. But that idea was becoming too unwieldy. Percentages don't work well in real life with its messy heaps. Percentages are best suited to abstract areas, like pure math, or science. Least of all with art.

How could people accurately divide up a trove of paintings? You could divide up a farm of chickens, where each one is alike, but not paintings. That would be more of a crapshoot.

But, apparently, it's done. This awkward division of quality rather than quantity.

But dividing quantity is hard enough in the real world. Riley thought about the time Rebecca and he tried to split up their possessions. She had moved out of their jointly owned house and was living with another man. She came over to the now broken home and they calmly decided to separate their possessions.

They sat down at the kitchen table.

"Okay," he said. "Take your pick."

"All right. I'll have this soup spoon." A collectible enamelled large soup spoon.

"One soup spoon for you. I suppose we should put it in a pile. I'll have . . . this tea pot."

An early 20th Century hand painted porcelain Chinese tea pot. They had a collection of them, around twenty.

"I'll have one, too." Rebecca said.

"This is going to take a long time."

They had a pile of goods that they'd moved from Canada to Florida. It was a rather large amount of antiques and inexpensive bric a brac. Daunting.

"It is."

He didn't remember how they abandoned the idea. Who did what. But they ended up having sex in the downstairs bedroom. It was the last time they ever tried anything remotely like it. Maybe Rebecca was cleverly demonstrating how ridiculous such a plan was.

Riley was genuinely confused, but the sex helped clear up many issues. Sex had a way of straightening things out. His feelings became less foggy. Good and bad, beautiful and ugly, truth and falsehood: sex was able to pinpoint and distinguish between each of these realities. It brought vague things into the light. After sex he knew himself better, and what he wanted and didn't want to happen.

They lived very individual, imaginative lives, and were willing to try out many paths as a result. And to leave just as many and go in a different direction.

If you never attempt anything, how can you really be sure about that thing? Riley always felt he had plenty of time for his little experiments. They were worth it. They led to concrete understanding.

He'd get busy on his stupid will. It was the adult thing to do. But Riley valued the child in him. It was still very much alive and kicking. Adult things were often merely corrupt, brainless things. But it wasn't always easy to decide what should be undertaken, and what simply solved itself if you ignored it and gave it some extra time.

The next time he met with Oliver they'd talk it over and Riley would cross all the tees and dot every i. He was becoming an adult at the end of a long, hard road. And he wasn't applauding the fact. It was mostly a sordid business. And it could even spell disaster for a genuine artist. Something that's a bit of a paradox.

He wondered how he was different from the great majority of humanity. In some ways, yes. But nothing extraordinary. He wasn't in a class by himself. He understood that. No matter what he did or thought of doing, there were others doing the same.

But he tried to make it clear, at least to himself.

Imagine getting up in the morning and realizing that today you need to do something that's never been done before. By anyone, ever, including yourself. That your whole essence depends on this trait, this summons to singularity. The pressure is turned up high. Balls to the wall.

It might feel better to stay in bed, with the covers wrapped tightly around your dozing cabeza.

But that will not happen.

And then imagine that this call from beyond . . . this ferocious need . . . is something that occurs every day for over fifty years. Yes. What a life. What a disturbing life. But this is precisely the life that Riley has chosen.

4.

He painted, and stopped. Once again, it was anything but a source of gladness in his soul. Once again his intentions were foiled. Unable to be concretely, objectively, accomplished. This same feeling has tormented him each day of his peculiar existence.

If you knock yourself out for so long maybe it wasn't the right path for you. Maybe it was all a stupendous error of judgment. One interminable self-hatched affliction.

However, with each painful thought that gnawed at him Riley also had other thoughts that wiped the bitterness away. Enthusiasm was followed by despair followed by new enthusiasm. Over and over.

He was reading Spinoza. He'd picked up a book at the thrift store. The great philosopher's basic writings. Riley hadn't read Spinoza for many decades. He decided on reading some unfamiliar part. The letters.

Lately he'd come to this conclusion. Do not reread anything. What was the point? You got whatever you were able to get from the first reading. Move on. There are other things to investigate. The original read had its effect. Leave it alone. And open something new.

There are 130 million books that have been published. Isn't that enough for you?

Yesterday was Kristina's birthday. Raphael, his mother, and Riley all decided on going out for dinner to celebrate. Each wrote down their choice, and they put them in a hat and drew one out. It was grandpa's: Wurstkuche, the German-styled beirstube restaurant in Little Tokyo. Customized hot dogs, home fries, and imported beer.

"Have you ever read Stephen Hawking, grandpa?" Raphael asked as they drove.

"I have. Something about the nature of time."

"'A Brief History of Time' Did you like it?"

"I did. But I can't remember much of it."

"It was about black holes."

Riley was more and more mystified at his grandson's comments. He never knew what was coming next. He now had pretty good idea who would inherit his library after he croaked.

Kristina took a photo of Riley and Raphael walking. He was surprised to notice that there was no longer such a difference in their respective heights.

"Either I am shrinking or he's shooting up," he said to Kristina. "Probably both."

Kristina then wanted a photo of her and her son. Riley obliged. Instead of a still he took about a dozen seconds of video, which she could edit later. She looked happier than ever.

The dinner was adequate, but Raphael was still a little miffed that Cole's, his oddly favorite restaurant in all of L. A., wasn't drawn out of the hat. His mother promised that they'd go soon. As a reward for his remarkably good report card. A perfect 4.0. No one in the family can understand it.

It was a fun evening although Riley was uncharacteristically less talkative. His mind was filled with two issues. He wanted to get back to the studio to ruminate silently and at length.

It was something new for him. Having less and less to add to the conversation in social gatherings. Even though tonight it was only the three of them, and as close to the family core as you could get. Three generations. And the only representatives of Riley's genetic line. A thin golden thread. How much longer would it last on this earth?

What were the issues buzzing in Riley's head? First, painting problems. Last, new insights as a result of a passage in one of Spinoza's letters. Both assailed him, to the point where he was in danger of being a wet blanket on his daughter's birthday festivities. He bravely held up his end of the stick and returned home.

He wanted to once again incorporate words on his latest painting. But his hand lettering was ugly. It stuck out like an ape wearing a tuxedo. It was unnatural for him. Something maybe from way back in his upbringing. He couldn't understand his disgust with his hand writing, especially as it appeared on his painting.

It was exacerbated by his awareness of Rebecca's skill in this area. She was an expert calligrapher. She'd learned the technique probably in architecture school where she was asked to do renderings. Riley loved seeing her work, even today, where she made small ink sketches, complete with quotations. Some of which she took from his own scribblings.

He splashed fresh paint over his grotesque attempts at writing on his newest painting.

But the idea of words on his visual art was not something to be abandoned for good. Especially in light of a concept he came up with a few days ago. A better way of working. Simply take lines from his novels and spread them across the surface.

Actually, he found an even more interesting line that he didn't create. It was from a zen story. It would be best to relate the entire translation:

"The zen master Hakuin was praised by his neighbours as one living a pure life.

A beautiful Japanese girl whose parents owned a food store lived near him. Suddenly, without any warning, her parents discovered that she was with child.

This made her parents angry. She would not confess who the man was, but after much harassment at last named Hakuin.

In great anger the parents went to the master. 'Is that so?' was all he would say.

After the child was born it was brought to Hakuin. By this time he had lost his reputation, which did not trouble him, but he took very good care of the child. He obtained milk from his neighbors and everything else he needed.

A year later the girl-mother could stand it no longer. She told her parents the truth - the real father of the child was a young man who worked in the fish market.

The mother and father of the girl at once went to Hakuin to ask forgiveness, to apologize at length,and to get the child back.

Hakuin was willing. In yielding the child, all he said was: 'Is that so?'"

Riley felt that he couldn't improve on this story. He was pleased with the translated
words. *Is that so.* They would look great stretched across his painting. But by using the individual silkscreens he owned.

Twenty-six letters, each burned on a separate screen. He'd been using them for around ten years, off and on. He wanted to make a new set but it would have cost too much. At least for now he would stick with what's there.

The next one would use a larger sized alphabet. Maybe a different font. Maybe even a font of his own design. Or perhaps Rebecca's design. Why not? New fonts were being developed all the time.

The story of the monk who was unfairly accused and who handled it with superb nonchalance struck Riley as something extraordinary and need to be committed to memory.

It had the ring of truth. Maybe it was artistically edited and altered from the literal facts, but that didn't make it less meaningful.

To experience injustice without squawking at the top of your lungs, everywhere and to everyone, would be something worthy of embracing. Riley was aware how far he was from doing this. Whenever something seemed even a little bit unfair he was quick to mention it. To portray himself as a victim.

So mediocre, and commonplace. The story made him ashamed of his actions.

He showed it to Kristina, who read it while he got up and had a glass of water.

"A great story," she concurred.

"But why am I so unlike this heroic monk? I'm forced to admit it."

"He's very rare."

"Right, and we have a belief in rarity. Even if our behavior isn't always so rare."

"We believe that true love is rare."

"We do."

"And my girl friends hate it when I say so."

"Why would that be?"

"I'm not sure. But I know they hate the idea."

"I think maybe because they want to feel that love is everywhere and all they have to do is grab the first person that comes along. Their goal is to blend in with the crowd, and the crowd is made up of very ordinary, average, completely unoriginal people. They aspire to erase any differences that keep them from being comfortably united with the
masses. Someone wrote that humans seek comfort, not knowledge."

"Jessica would be completely happy with a man who comforted her day and night."

"Really? You mean she has no interest in a life devoted to learning."

"I know she's never read a book. And never will. She most definitely would choose comfort over knowledge."

"And over rarity, too. She must like these ordinary men because she conceives herself that way. She doesn't believe in her rarity, and how rare it would be to find another as rare as herself."

5.

Riley plunged into a meditation on the many close calls he's had in this world. How he could easily have had a child with some tremendously ordinary women. But how instead he had a child with Rebecca, who is the least ordinary woman he's ever known.

These close calls made him sweat blood when reviewing them. How some invisible force led him away from his dreadful choices.

This thought gave way to something he just read in Spinoza. Riley loved philosophy almost as much as art, but he was not as gifted in this intellectual field. The only thing that seemed to be on his side was his ability to hammer away at many of the difficult questions he found there.

Spinoza tried to clarify for his correspondent the problem of privation, or loss. Something that Riley had been studying for decades. How such a thing as loss, absence, or lack, could exist. Spinoza pointed out that it was not something found in nature, but rather it was a purely mental construction based on comparisons.

This was a knotty problem that Riley tried to see clearly. He had a flash of an example. It seemed to come out of nowhere. He saw two pieces of square wood placed next to each other. One was a pure block. The other had a whole all the way through it.

Why would someone say that one piece of wood was lacking something, like a plug to fill the hole? Why didn't they think the block was complete, even with a hole? Wasn't it simply a judgement based on comparison with a holeless block next to it?

Wouldn't it be just as meaningful to say the smooth block was lacking a hole drilled through it? Lack, or privation, was an idea, not a factual condition present in the object.

To assert that something utterly complete the way it is, is actually incomplete and imperfect is, well, a strange interpretation. Nothing is missing. All is there. But human beings will make a mental judgment to the contrary.

This simple observation has so many ramifications. Spinoza, a kind of extreme pantheist, would say that the two blocks of wood are both perfect and complete as far as it is in their nature to be so.

Although Riley struggled to understand Spinoza, he nevertheless got something of his own out of the man's writing. A better, fuller, more concrete understanding of the truth concerning privation, negation, lack, absence, and all ideas about the phenomenon known as "missing." When something, or someone, is described as missing something that they must have, such as a spouse or lover.

This new knowledge could apply to Riley's painting and writing style, as well as his social, and ethical behavior. It had a lot to do with a lot.

"I still need to make sense of what people mean by "missing", he said to his daughter.

"I know. It's just something people say, or sometimes they actually feel it."

"You mean if a person tells you that they miss you, they don't really mean it?"

"They don't if sex is not involved."

"So we never really miss someone except if we have sexual feelings for them. That sounds really odd. But it does make sense."

"You said it yourself. You missed Sara when you were in the army, and missed Rebecca when you were away from her. When you took me to California when I was two."

"True. The only time I ever missed anyone was when they were my lover. But missing can expand to cover a lot of areas. We miss home because that's where our sexuality thrives. I shouldn't feel bad that I don't miss my friends or family. I never missed my parents. I only missed a woman I wanted sex with."

"And I only missed a man I wanted sex with."

"But do you think we're just eccentric, or cold-hearted? And too sexually obsessed?"

"We could be seeing it more clearly than other people. Chloe feels like we do."

"So if a woman ever admits that she misses me I should know what she really means."

"She wouldn't say that if she wasn't attracted to you."

"Probably. Or she could be out of touch with her own feelings."

"But not completely. The attraction won't allow to be blind to her emotions."

"Funny, but Sartre argued that there's no such thing as a subconscious mind. We always know what's going on in our head even if we try to hide it from ourselves, and bury it in some dark corner."

"That makes sense to me. It leaks out and exposes our secrets."

"But they're never that secret to ourselves."

"No. I notice if a person is grumbling and complaining about something and if I was to ask them what they were thinking about five minutes ago they'd likely have to admit it was about someone they'd want sex with. But something was in the way of that happening."

"So all frustration comes down to that. I think we're even taking beyond what Freud thought."

"I know. It's a hard sell."

"I can't imagine who would accept it. But that doesn't make it false."

"No, we could just be early adopters of that interpretation."

"I see it this way. The world is sentimental. That means instead of zeroing in on the real cause of its misery it builds this huge mushroom cloud of socially acceptable reasons behind their feelings. They dilute the truth so it fills the air with all these benign fairy tales, evasions, and indirect images."

"I can see how they like to do that."

"For example, this picture of a lonely soldier boy in his foxhole on Christmas Eve. How he says he misses the dining room table, the laughter, the opening of presents, his brothers and sisters, the whole spirit of that distant place called home. It's not that it's a falsification of his feelings, but it's rather that they're too watered down and made more childishly innocent. What he really misses is his girlfriend and their naked passion. That's his home inside of his home."

"I agree, but it's still a hard sell."

"Not for me, and others like me."

"I was at the gym yesterday and I caught the eye of this really handsome man that I've been telling you about."

"Okay. That's good."

"Well, sort of. But a few minutes later I look over and he's standing at the far end and yawning. Really yawning."

"Not a good sign. For you."

"A terrible sign. Do I ever feel tired when I'm in the presence of someone I desire? Never. I'm wide awake. Wired!"

"These things are rarely so synchronized. But sometimes you notice hints. From now on if a woman ever mentions the fact that she misses something about me I will go on high alert."

"Only if you are equally attracted to her."

"Or maybe I just wasn't aware of her feelings, but now I am. Maybe it's different for a woman."

"It is. Men aren't so inclined to hide what they feel about me. I can be fooled about whether or not they want to get married, but not be their desire for sex."

"I see. You can tell if a man wants to go part of the way with you, but not all the way."

"Something like that."

"I'm kind of glad I never pretended that I ever wanted anything more than to make love to a woman. I never dangled any offers to her beyond that. At least I didn't add hypocrisy to my other sins."

"I suppose you could congratulate yourself on that."

Kristina didn't sound as if she was happy to hear this about her father. Not his noblest admission. It must have confused some women.

"It's funny when I last talked to that interior designer, the one I think is so beautiful, I told her I missed working with her. How phony is that? I miss not having sex with her."

"That you even chose to use the word is very revealing."

"It definitely is. I would never use that word if I was talking to someone unappetizing. Certainly not to a man. But it's never really been that clear to me before today."

Talking things over with an open-minded person, if you are as open-minded, can be very useful.

6.

Riley was a little upset when he saw the time. He'd slept in this morning. 9:23. But, after all, it was Sunday. No one was coming by early. Yesterday the two Hispanic woodworkers had dropped off a couple of tabletops. For Kristina.

He didn't have any money for them. She hadn't left a check.

"Okay, then, on Monday?" One of the men asked, smiling.

"I'm sure, by then."

People always want to get paid as soon as they can. They look forward to it, and dream about what they'll do with the money. Riley was really like that. He had very little trust in people who owed him money.

No one likes to pay up. Everyone is slow to reach into their pocket and hand over a big wad of cash. It's only natural. This movement of exchange.

Money is real, but what you buy is questionable. To let go of something real for what might not be as real makes for some anxious moments.

Seen from another angle to present something in the hope of receiving money for it also

creates anxiety. Is it good enough? Am I charging enough, or too much? Too little? What if they don't want it, and back out of the deal?

So much of Riley's life was spent suffering from these everyday concerns. Silent undercurrents flowing through hidden conduits. Barely felt, but always there. Like trains deep underground vibrating on the surface as they move along.

How could it be otherwise, Riley wondered. This arcane system of credit for efforts. If you worked you could supposedly eat, and have a roof over your head. And cover yourself with clothing. The bare necessities for a human existence.

And Riley did work. And was still working. Even if many people his age no longer did. And hadn't done so for several years.

This was one of the chief reasons why he overslept today. He had painted last night. Until around one o'clock.

One in the morning wasn't that late. Not for a lot of people.
Mostly young.

In fact as he turned off the lights in the studio he could still
hear the guitar and drums playing across the alley. Some
kids lived there, and had their own band.

Riley's industrial fan cancelled out the sounds of a band
performing, or maybe practising. It was hard to tell.

And he was tired enough to fall asleep without too much
tossing beforehand.

At least it was better than being out stealing cars, he thought.
The kids playing, or trying to play music.

The woodworkers, even though they were still smiling, didn't
push off immediately after unloading the extra long tabletops.

"I like that one," a man said, pointing at a painting stacked
against the wall.

But then Kristina appeared. She must have received a phone
call from her team of workers.

Riley went to the back of the studio while she settled up with them. Dishing out their money.

"Could you move your truck, so they can leave?" she said to her dad.

After that they sat down, and Riley drank his coffee.

"I think $350 is too much for the wood," she said.

"The wood only for those two tops? Way too much."

"I know. I'll have to say something next time."

Riley thought about it for a few seconds.

"But they do save you a lot of time and hassle. Going there and choosing the wood. Plus it's really fine. It never warps, and I love the knotholes."

"It stains beautifully."

"When I was really knocking them out. When I was shipping them to Europe and all over LA, I used to start every week driving over to Rudolpho's and giving him a check for $600. Every week. Just for the stretchers and plastered canvas.

But it was worth it, and I never thought twice about it, when Inga and I piled a dozen into the pickup. I can't imagine doing that again. But when you're really cooking you don't bat an eyelid."

"Maybe that's my problem. I'm selling, but not enough."

"You have an ongoing business, whether you know it or not."

"I don't see it getting any bigger. But I understand what you're saying."

"If things just keep happening as they are it'll be good for us both. I mean your tables and my paintings. Even if I don't sell mine, and the people in the front room keep paying the rent."

Riley was banking on his tenants staying put. He'd recently seen the improvements in the other half of his building and was blown away. It was transformed, mainly by the addition of skylights. So impressive. Today it looked like something featured in a design magazine.

And they were paying him to live there, on top of fixing up the joint. Even if they moved out it'd be easy to rent again. Probably easier, now that it looked so good.

"Any news from our gang?" he asked.

"Nothing, really. That movie! What a piece of shit. And three hours long. I told Raphael that's enough. No more movies for me."

"I heard it got terrible reviews. I didn't want to mention it. Figuring it would only make it worse for you."

"And it's funny because I know the director. He came up to me at Erewon and seemed so interested. Then I ran into him again and he said he tried to find our business but he couldn't. He's handsome. He likes me. Why shouldn't I go out with him? But then I saw his film!"

"Well, maybe he'll make other ones."

"Not after this bomb. Also heard from Ellie. She complained about her date. Always the same thing with her. She doesn't need a friend. She needs a man. They don't want anything sexual with her. Just the opposite of Jessica. With her they only want sex and nothing else. And then they're gone forever."

"I was thinking about that and had this insight. Pleasure and pain are commonplace. Everyone experiences that. But true love is rare."

"Exactly. It's like what Marcel told you about relationships."

"Relationships are always about pleasure and pain? Delirium and tears? But have nothing to do with true love?"

"Yes, that must have been why he was so negative about relationships."

"Now it all makes sense to me. At the time I couldn't figure out why he was so down on relationships. It was because I was floundering around in them."

7.

Riley thought about the last conversation with his daughter. The part where they separated two distinct human activities. Relationships, and True Love. He then tried to come up with a suitable image. A large, misshapen, grey boulder with a small, faceted, sparkling emerald resting on top.

The difference in size and value seemed right.

Relationships are commonplace. Everyone has them by the handful. You couldn't escape them. A person's life is a web of clumsy entanglements.

True love was set apart from these unavoidable encounters. It is incomparable. A matter of quality, not quantity. It is something everyone admires and longs for, but is so strangely magical and veiled. Riley thought of it like ghosts, aliens, or flying saucers. People talked about them, believed in them, but very seldom saw them.

Riley wasn't sure that true love was merely a grand illusion.

After all, he could say he hadn't really ever known it. He believed it was one of those things that you couldn't fail to understand if you were really swept into its reality. Nor could you mistake something else for it, or it for something else.

But all this was only carefully reasoned guesswork. He admitted that he was in the thickest darkness when it came to true love.

But he had faith in its existence. It was something that held great promise for those who vainly sought it. Maybe it's essentially imperceptible from the outside.

He then analyzed his own life. His world, from start to finish. What if it was only what he was able to partially experience? The rest remaining in obscurity, and unknown.

Everything beyond his cone of vision had no real existence for him. It was anyone's guess what it was. Riley was unable to penetrate the wall of his being.

Or what if true love was something like a country that he was barred from entering? An island somewhere, out of reach, perhaps imaginary. Rumors reached his ears, but nothing more.

All of his friends, family, lovers, even people he passed on the street, were unable to demonstrate the real presence of that bewitching phantom he called true love. Everyone who he made contact with was unable to offer him proof of what he was investigating.

He sensed that he would know it when he actually saw it. Or better, when he felt it. Up to this point it was only something secondhand. He had no way to tell the real thing from its copy. He wasn't even sure that a copy was in fact a copy. Whatever it was, it couldn't be what he was after.

"Philippe just texted. He said he read your novel."

"Oh, man. I can confirm that I sold one book in Great Britain. It had to be the one he purchased."

Riley had no interest in having people examine what he may have written about them. He had to write about this or that individual, and to do it in a way that he found acceptable. He wasn't selling anyone a portrait in words.

He didn't feel like saying anything except what was on his mind and his fingertips as he typed. There wasn't much censorship involved. And this might lead to some wounded feelings. Then again, it may not. How could he tell?

If a writer wasn't being honest, what did he think he was doing? A dishonest writer wasn't a writer at all. He was a mere hack, confused, very short-sighted. Typewriting, but not writing.

Riley felt threatened by those he wrote about, under assumed names, and disguised circumstances. It was only a few degrees from the real thing. The most laughably transparent costume. Anyone from his scene who read his books could spot at a glance the source of his characters.

But they were in fact only one-dimensional re-creations. They were not flesh and blood humans. Mere figments of his imagination. Thin air. He didn't succeed in bringing them to life. He wasn't gifted enough for that. But he was able to fill many pages with his fanciful jottings. Many couldn't do that much. And some of them are actual authors with decent reputations.

"It's as if the only people who read your books are the ones you don't want to read them."

"But that can't last, can it? I mean books go on, but we all die. I also realize why certain people no longer feel right about talking with me. Eva, for instance, even though she's never read one of my novels, suspects how I go about it. She senses that I'd write down her words whatever they may be."

"So a person can't even object, or they'll see their objections in print?"

"Something like that. I guess it's my style, like it or not. But so what? If I have a conversation with anyone they have a right to put it in print. Maybe as long as they change my name and a few other minor circumstances about me. I think the law bears me out. There's nothing illegal about creating something. None that I can think of. It's called artistic license. Freedom of expression, a constitutional right."

"But do people care what's being written about them? Even if it's the truth? I think Philippe needs to hear certain things about himself."

"You mean that he's not always helping himself out? But he doesn't see it that way."

"No, but I think it's good for him. He's a little too cocky. And you can imagine how he described me to his goofy, rich chums."

"That could be. So, we're all characters in some person's book, even if we never get to read it."

"At least I finally dated a man who can read a book," she said.

"Yes, and I have a novel that exists in the land where Shakespeare lived. But Philippe probably won't text you again. Because whatever he says may end up in another novel."

"But why should that be a bad thing?"

"I don't know. I guess people want to control the way they appear. They want to be portrayed as they see themselves in their fantasies. Not through another person's filter. People think I distore them. Maybe I do. But not as much as they distort themselves."

"You couldn't really stop someone from having their own ideas about themselves. And about your descriptions."

"That's true. Even if they never mentioned it out loud. I'm free to have my own thoughts. No one can prevent that. I'm sure there are plenty of people who have the meanest, most rancid, opinion of me. I'd be shocked to know it. But this is the way life is lived. You can always shoot yourself if it becomes unbearable. The door is open."

Everyone has their stories, and you are part of these stories. Nor do you get to choose which role you play. Sometimes you're the hero, sometimes the villain. But however you're cast you're likely to be included in the drama.

"My dream lover at the gym finally spoke to me," she said.

Riley noticed a little difference in his daughter this morning. She smiled more, and there was some fresh color in her cheeks. It reminded him of her mother. Rebecca always appeared flushed when she responded to the attention of a new man in her life. It must mean that there was some trigger in their shared blood. It leapt in their veins. It was the case for Chloe, too. She turned rose red.

When it happened with Rebecca, Riley was alarmed. He knew he wasn't the cause of this visible rush of feeling. But with the daughters it only made him happy. He supposed it was the difference between romantic desire and fatherly love. He liked to see Kristina's life brightened and made joyful, even if it was only temporary.

Transitory love is still love, and it's nothing to deride.

"Well, what did he say?"

"Nothing at all, but at least he was the one who spoke first."

"Good for you. That must have taken some intense self-control."

"It did, but I'm glad he broke the ice. He said 'here, let me move those towels for you.'"

"Not exactly a declaration of undying love, but something concrete."

"I don't know why it's so important. For a woman not to speak first."

"Very odd, but true. Like one of those things that go back to our legacy as animals. Hard to rebel against.

"But some women do. Like Ellie. She just marches right up to a strange man and starts babbling. But maybe that's why nothing ever works out for her."

"Your mom once told me a peculiar story. She was in New York by herself and sitting down at a restaurant and began a conversation with a table of men. She wanted to know if any of them knew one of her old classmates when he went to school in Manhattan. They did and gave her his number. She went out with him later, and he said the men at the other table thought she was a hooker."

"Because she started the conversation?"

"I don't know. Probably. Seems unfair, doesn't it?"

"Yes, but that's the way it is in our culture. I think it must be especially the case if the woman is good-looking."

"That could be."

"I don't imagine men would think a big fat loony woman who spoke to them would be a prostitute."

"No. Or a very aged woman."

"But to be forced to wait calmly until a man breaks the silence is disturbing. Even though I'm really glad I did."

"I'm not even sure why it's necessary and important. Except the results speak for themselves. I know that I was the first one to speak to your mother, although I don't remember what I said."

"We said it a lot of the time it was about shyness, and overcoming shyness."

"Women are allowed to be shy in this case, and men have to summon up some reserve of boldness."

"But not if a man is just naturally bold and isn't reluctant to approach any woman all day long. His feelings aren't involved, and he doesn't care in the least if he's rejected. He just goes on to the next woman. Obliviously."

"I'm a bit shy and if a woman rejects me it's enough to make me run and hide for at least a year. It really strikes deep. I can't believe how much I take it to heart and suffer from it."

"Rainer was that way. He had to get some other man to come along on our first date. He really battled with his shyness."

"But then again if I have a few drinks I can swagger with the best of them. I must have two people inside my brain. I still find it weird. What drugs or booze can do to a man."

"Or a woman, too. I guess shy people are helped by these crutches."

"Not really. It keeps them from ever becoming who they genuinely are. Someone who can act directly without any artificial props. When a woman has to get drunk to have sex with me I know she's repulsed by me. But something is stronger than her disgust."

"It's how I feel about Philippe. A lot about him is a big turn off, but he at least is handsome."

"Like when Eva says I'm good-looking but need to improve my hygiene."

"Right. You can be cleaned up, and so sex isn't impossible."

"I wonder if Aylish will ever reach that point? If she stops the drugs, the chain smoking, the junk food, bad politics, and religious fundamentalism. Man, the list goes on. But at least she's still pretty much a young woman."

"What about the schizophrenia? You said that's a bridge too far."

"But I'm no doctor. And didn't Raphael say that even mentally ill people still need love?"

"He did."

"I never imagined that I'd be taking advice from my grandchild. I can't see my grandfather ever doing that. He would have been crazy to, in my case."

Riley was thankful for the conversations he had with his intelligent daughter. He liked intelligence wherever he found it. Mostly in men, but also in women.

He read something a woman once wrote: some women are smarter than most men. He readily agreed. It was a modest way of putting it. Any yokel might agree with the assertion. Only a purebred knucklehead would doubt it.

The intelligent women he met in his life came and went. Only a few stuck around for long. So most of the pertinent remarks from this category of women were brief. Like darts that occasionally hit him out of the blue.

His daughter, however, was there for decades. Even Rebecca didn't match her child in this respect. Riley had many useful talks with Rebecca. Very enlightening, but they were now in second place and well behind Kristina.

"I always say that I learned a lot more from your mother than she learned from me."

"You might want to keep that to yourself," she said.

"But it's true. A New York woman can impart a great deal to a curiously minded man from Iowa. With cornstalks sticking out of his collar. It isn't exactly a two way street. Nor should it be."

Riley had reached another circle of attainment. That's what he decided to call this periodic movement in his life. It felt like a series of concentric rings, with abrupt shifts from one to the next.

These sudden changes always left him speechless and a bit shaky. Like someone landing in a new foreign country. It took some time to find his way. To move from mystified tourist to fully established citizen.

Today was no different, and just as bewildering. No point in denying it. For decades he'd been making his modest living by jumping out of bed in the morning and going to work creating stuff to be sold.

But today that process, that life-style, came to an unexpected halt. He no longer needed to make things that brought in enough cash to keep a roof over his head. He actually could get by doing nothing. Jack shit. Simply staring out the window for hours at a time. The roof would remain, and everything would stream by as usual. Without his physical efforts.

It was very uncanny. Hard to understand clearly. The result was a gradual, but radical, new adjustment. This movement was felt in every pore. Profoundly so. He was old, but somehow new at the same time.

 It felt like a mathematician checking his figures over and over, but having to finally accept the validity of the equation. It was real, and it was true. All is now, and will be in the future, different. Acknowledge it. He'd be crazy not to. By degrees, slowly, he began to let in sink in.

How many circles did he traverse in his 78 years on this earth? He wasn't sure.   A few, but not that many. Somewhere between five and ten, perhaps. If they were significant enough to count.

Nor were they clearly marked off. Not sharply delineated. They might overlap, here and there.

These circles might not be like the ones that appear when a rock is thrown into a pond. That is, ever widening outwards. They could be like arms and fingers closing around a point.

Riley tended to believe they were both movements carried on simultaneously. Greater outwardness combined with deeper inwardness. He sensed himself becoming larger and smaller in harmony.

Before he went to bed last night he examined the painting he'd been working on. It depressed him. It was a flop. There was no way he'd be able to fall asleep while it was in this present state of ugliness.

He got up, turned on the lights and started furiously painting. Covering nearly everything he'd done over a week. Until it was nearly all white. At that point he stopped and climbed back into bed. And slept soundly.

The choices were now clearer than they'd ever been. The wrong and right way to go. The wrong path was like a punch in the mouth. The right path was like the sweetest kiss. Why wasn't it always so crystal clear?

Who could say? But at least it was at this moment. And that was something to be thankful for.

"That was nice of you to put up Rebecca's art on your Instagram page," Riley said.

"Yeah. I liked the quote. And the painting."

She quoted a passage from Dante, the father of the Renaissance, and one of Riley's heroes. For years he tried to figure out how to paint a vast canvas of the Divine Comedy.

Hell would be peopled by mostly modern tyrants and depraved men and women. Serial killers, rapists, war-mongers. Purgatory would be full of fence-sitters. The famous types who had one foot in evil and the other in goodness. Paradise would tower over the other two sections. Riley had plenty of superior humans who would be sitting around, basking in light and glory.

He really didn't feel equal to the task. So it remained on the back burner for many years. Maybe someday. Maybe he could portray it more imaginatively. But he didn't give up on the idea.

His own art was milder, less judgmental. He knew who belonged where. Who would be damned and worthy of violent suffering. But he held off on pinning them down in his art. If anything he concentrated on the noble men and women who filled this world with sublime values. His heaven would be crammed with recognizable names. But his hell would almost be deserted. A sad, lonely desolation.

It was so easy to become fucked up. Riley empathized with the contemptible wretches. They deserved to shriek in agony. But he was nearly more inclined to wipe the blood from their sweating brows than to stoke the infernal flames. Evil was its own reward.

Riley was inclined toward mercy. He couldn't even comprehend why. It was unjust. He'd make a lousy judge. He never sat on a jury, even though he'd received a number of summons to do so. He always tossed them in the trash.

He believed that time was like a powerfully confusing drug. It meant trying to make your way through a jungly maze, beset by unsuspected obstacles at every step. Each explorer was rocked and shaken. Many ended by nearly destroying their vulnerable souls. Time was a soaring challenge, even for the best. No wonder everyone had stumbled and failed.

Riley was now re-studying Spinoza. Even the name had a magical ring. Spinoza. He found some images of this remarkable philosopher. His portraits showed a thoughtful, somewhat handsomely intelligent face, which was a surprise.

Riley had always thought of him as heavier and more bourgeois. This was not at all the case. And the Jewish "God-drunk" philosopher died at the early age of 44. He lived a very Spartan life, and it coincided with his own system of explanation.

So, his life wasn't one thing and his philosophy something else. Which is the way Riley saw most intellectual types. In fact hardly anyone lived their truths.

"I like Spinoza. He tried to give a systematic explanation to our feelings. He logically described how they operated. And that theyre 'so much more powerful than our rationality."

"I'll have to read him," said Kristina.

"I've always believed that no one can fully tame their emotions. All attempts to do so are only partly successful. We're like wild animals in a flimsy cage. We're kept locked up due to laziness, fear, and a kind of fateful indifference. We all belong to an organization of prisoners. The prison bosses tell us to stay put, and we obey."

"I try hard to be a stoic, but I'm not that good at it."

"No one is. Stoicism is an ideal, and not a reality. Spinoza says we're all part of a long chain of causes, and our freedom consists only in realizing this necessary truth. We can at least observe ourselves interpreting this situation. That's as free as it can be."

"I'm not sure I understand."

"Neither do I. It's as if you're free to the extent that you understand how unfree you are when you're just living without grasping the necessary truth of your plight. I'm free when I identify myself with necessary cause of all life."

Riley saw that he wasn't making much sense, and stopped talking. They changed the subject, but he still tried to answer this question in the silent moments that followed.

Freedom was eternal life, which was uncreated. It was always around. Always present. A human being was free when he transformed himself in accord with the essence of life itself. It was a point where necessity and freedom fused.

Looked at from one angle necessity was like an iron vise crushing a person. But from another it was like a perfectly orderly evolution. Similar to Neitzsche's "dancing in chains."

Riley believed he was free when he adjusted himself to the hidden rhythms of universal reality. Everything except that was a type of ignominious, semi-conscious slavery.

Slavery was the antithesis of creativity. An artist is never a slave. They are free or they are not artists.

This is the stage where today Riley found himself. Everything in the past, all his labor, was alienated, or the product of his thralldom. In short, artifacts, but not art. Commodities, objects, things, hand-crafted items - but not art.

This fresh insight signalled a change. He was compelled by his own new understanding to radically change how he went about his life. He could not defy his clarified vision. Without ceasing to be who he is.

"I received a phone call from the guy in Orange County. I refused to answer it."

"Good."

"I will not slip back into the old, slavish ways. Never!"

He knew what the man wanted. Some family portraits. But Riley wasn't about to grant him his wish. He'd made an irrevocable decision. Come hell or high water. Irreversible. All the way to the edge of doom.

"This is something unprecedented. I feel it in the marrow of my bones. To have no sales, and no romance. Nothing to distract me from painting. No sales, but it doesn't matter. I no longer need them. I can exist without them. Never happened before."

Riley was experiencing his long deferred freedom. The attainment of his full maturity as a creative being. It made him tremble with mysterious dread.

Kristina recalled how nervous she was a few years ago when she was starting to design and fabricate her tables.

"I couldn't fall asleep at night. I was so worried that people wouldn't like them. But today it's not like that at all. I was relaxed about that $10,000 sale, and wasn't the least bit freaked out."

"Because you've mastered the ability to build and sell your product. You're an entrepreneur. You started a business from scratch. Many people want to do this. Some will actually try, and then fail."

"I suppose I have."

"But here is something odd. An artist never feels that kind of relief. Because he can't make something that he can then repeat with no more aggravation. He can never put his calling on auto-pilot. What he did has nothing to do with what he will do. It's useless knowledge. Every day he has to begin all over again. He's the absolute beginner."

"It must make an artist depressed, and not look forward to the next day."

"Exactly. Every day dawns with the artist facing unbearable odds. No wonder they seem so miserable and desperate. They're not businessmen, craftsmen, or entrepreneurs. They can't rely on their know-how. They can only count on creativity to make something new."

"So they have to go on blind faith?"

He shrugged.

Why, when people call for paintings . . . commission work . . . why can't he just say that practice is discontinued. When you see that word discontinued in a catalogue, you don't ask the business to make an exception for you. It really feels final. From now on he'll only paint what inspires him.

He opened up Spinoza. Riley had such a limited mentality, and it was becoming more so by the day. But at least philosophy was less opaque to him. Spinoza wrote about freedom and necessity, and how they fit together. It was something that Riley had understood for a long time.

Did he get the idea originally from Spinoza almost fifty years ago? Or was it something he came up with on his own? He didn't know. But he was aware that he saw the philosopher's point.

Take a rock, for instance. It's neither living nor dead. It just is. You can pick it up and throw it as far as you want. It doesn't object. You can shove it around if it's small enough and you're strong enough.

But then consider people. You can't walk up to a stranger and give him a push. You might get slugged, or even arrested. Your freedom ends where his begins.

But you're free to tell him something. To push your opinions on him. Pushing a body is against the law, but pushing ideas is allowed. Maybe someday they won't be. The cops will be called if you try to shove your notions into a stranger's brain.

However, not all speech is legal. Threats, intimidation, harassment is illegal, and eventually some other forms will be outlawed as well.

Imagine a world where people are as sensitive about pushing ideas at each other as they are about jostling each other's bodies.

Riley would like to live in such a society. He feels he's ready for it. He wasn't in the past, but he is today.

"A thing is free which exists and acts solely by the necessity of its nature." Spinoza's definition of freedom.

Riley grasped it like never before. When he is wholly himself and acts that way, then he is free. But when external forces are applied and he bends under their pressure he is not free. These constraints needn't be present, but they can still do their work. They've left their imprint. And caused their damage.

All this is rather obvious. But Riley now realized that the freedom of his pure self also caused him to act in a necessary manner. A free man didn't behave capriciously, bizarrely, or arbitrarily. He conducted himself strictly as his nature demanded.

This discovery led to other questions. Why does a free person willingly act so necessarily? It feels like a compact unity. A special integration of two seemingly different realities:

what he's free to do is the same as what he needs to do. They both appear at once in a person's center.

What I need to do, I am free to do, and what I am free to do, I need to do, thought Riley. It was strange, this insight.

Most of his life there was a disjunction between his freedom and his needs. For example, he had imagined that he needed to live in Paris and become a painter, but he wasn't free to do it.

Or he was free to express his ideas about racial injustice, but he didn't need to waste his breath on this.

A disjunction. A separation. He didn't succeed in connecting the two activities.

These insights unveiled another truth as well. What about the unfree person? What is the fate of such a path? Doesn't the unfree man or woman have such a tragically different life?

The unfree types encumber themselves with unnecessary trifles. This unnecessary baggage can be suffocating. They load themselves with so many superfluities they can barely breathe. Due to their unfreedom they can't see what's necessary or not. Nor are they able to discern the need to be free. They've lost their way. They hardly know what's missing. Or how to pinpoint the solution.

Kristina handed her dad his last book. He finally had mailed her two copies. She kept one and gave him the other. He no longer cared to own any more. They were available if he was really curious about them.

"I like how this one turned out. It's slimmer, and the cover painting looks better. I think I prefer the glossy paper."

It was thinner because he scaled down the font size. There were several typos and misspellings due to his rushed style. He'd have to eventually correct them. But it was hard enough to get them into print without becoming a finicky editor. Let someone else handle that job. But who? They'd appear when the time was right.

"It looks less self-published," Kristina said.

"Right. I'm aware of all of its imperfections, but I'm still pleased that it's done at all."

He grabbed five novels and held them pressed together in one hand.

"This is how they'd look as one volume."

"Your own 'Remembrances of Things Past.'"

"Remembrances of things present. That's one of the differences. I prefer writing about the present."

"I like reading about our present."

"The past disgusts me. I've said it a thousand times. I wish people wouldn't take it personally. It's how a creative type might feel. I try to block out what was and concentrate on what is. Nor am I interested in what will be. I strive to live in the eternal now."

As a painter and a writer Riley didn't let himself become ensnared in previous phases of his lengthening life. He did his best, squeezed as much meaning out of his past as he could, and then moved on.

He didn't know whether this was a good idea or not. It was a choice.

But maybe Spinoza is right. Freedom for a human being isn't a choice, but rather a necessity. Riley was actively living his necessary liberation. He'd leave it at that. No more explanation was required. Even if he wasn't able to logically and rationally argue for his position, it wouldn't matter.

It was either a necessary free choice, or an unnecessary constrained choice. He hoped it was the former.

Riley wracked his brain. Yes, he was finally as free as he would ever be. But what could that mean for his art?

He stared at his latest painting. It once again looked like shit. He spent an hour covering most of the surface in white.

A day went by and then he covered the white in orange.

Late at night he started covering the orange, once more.

His freedom didn't guarantee success in art. What was the problem? Somehow the ideas of Spinoza intruded on his pondering. The freedom in painting wasn't different from the freedom in other areas of life. In love, politics, social life, etc. It was freedom that originated from a primal cause. Originated necessarily. Eternal freedom. Not the careless, fitful, trashy, stupid pseudo-freedom of fragmentary, partitioned life. Freedom in name only.

Not the so-called freedom of gangsters, violence, heartlessness, and misunderstanding.

Riley's painting had to take all these factors into account as he worked. His hands and eyes were one thing, coordinated with his adjustable mind. Painting freely needed to be one way, and not some other way.

It was very challenging. He kept muttering that it was time to give up. He had lost his lifelong fight. This feeling of giving up returned periodically. Today it was coming in the final rounds. He felt like a boxer who couldn't get off his stool, and was unable to answer the bell. Maybe it was time to throw in the towel.

What was necessary as a painting? Colors, shapes, words, lines, objects, figures, designs, etc.? Yes, but how to organize them all into something fresh and real and lasting? He really didn't know. Everything he'd previously done no longer seemed to be the answer.

His own paintings, all of them, were good only because they looked like other good paintings. This was a bitter puzzle. How could he make something good that didn't resemble other good things. Or how could it be good if it was merely an imitation of something else? Problems that he meditated on for decades, with varying success.

He felt he was closing in on the record for bad paintings. Over eleven thousand of them made and sold. It was a wonder he wasn't arrested. Having broken some obscure law.

But he was convinced that the answer to this conundrum was intimately connected with the question of freedom.

It was one of those weeks. He felt he needed a break.

He got one, right on schedule. Not the kind of break he wanted: a broken plumbing pipe in his studio. Somewhere under the floor of the bathroom. In the worst of places. It meant hiring a plumber. Not a single plumber, a whole crew of them. At a cost that made Riley destroy any illusions of possessing an adequate measure of stoic composure. It unnerved him. Even though he seemed outwardly calm and resigned.

"The floor under our bathroom has a pool of water," Bryce said. He was the male half of the couple who rented half of Riley's building. His girl friend was Mindy. Kristina said she was in her twenties, and maybe so was he. Good tenants.

Paying on the first of the month with a check that never bounces. Riley didn't delay.

"The plumbers are coming this weekend. Is that okay?" Could they wait a few days.

They could, and the crew arrived and set to work. Riley was prepared for them to find bigger problems once they removed the floor.

He was unfortunately right about that. Twice the original cost, but what can you do? The plumbers are like brain surgeons in middle of an operation. You had go along with them. They could pretty much name their price.

Riley stared at the rotten wood, and fractured pipe with water oozing from a break, creating a blackened lake of mud. It was probably that way for years. Riley had pretended that it was something that could be ignored. But he was only kidding himself and prolonging the inevitable.

He began working on the unfinished painting, as the plumbers walked by, to and from the alley.

The painting was going nowhere. His bank account once again treacherously low.

At least the final scab from the dermatologist came off. The skin cancer was apparently gone. No matter how many things happen in a day there's always a blend of the positive and negative.

Okay, the cost of the plumbing repair was steep, but he did have the money to pay. It could have been worse. He didn't have to borrow or use a credit card. And in a few days the friendly, quiet, responsible couple in the front room would hand him another check for a month's rent.

His skin cancer was gone. At least for now. He felt strong for his age. At least during the day. And not even repulsively ugly, according to flattering remark or two from attractive women.

The painting, too, was now coming along. He never had to throw away an overworked, ruined canvas. They always turned out even if it meant extra hours of work. He slashed away, and this sometimes proved successful. Delicate tinkering was never a good idea. It was always a mistake for Riley's style, which was bold and accomplished with speed.

He walked over to Kristina's house and aired his opinions about the present circumstances.

"It feels like another test. Are external difficulties going to send us over the edge? I remember how my father never complained about his business woes when he sat down at the table with us all for dinner. If he was angry and depressed he kept it to himself. He probably talked about it with our mother when the children went to bed. They spent a long time at the kitchen table speaking in lowered tones. But maybe even then he stopped himself from grumbling."

Riley wasn't the type to bottle up his displeasures. He let them fly toward anyone within earshot. He tried to express them in a way that might make people smile. Or at least have them realize that he wasn't about to pop his cork. He squawked, but half-humorously.

This is how he conducted himself in bad times. He was no zen master, or self-abasing monk with bowed head. But he didn't drive anyone crazy with his groaning. At least he hoped not.

8.

You are not responsible for everything. That would be too much for anyone. But you couldn't just close your eyes to external facts. Something out there depended on you, and your actions. Many things, however, were not your concern. Many more than Riley understood. He gave the world too much importance. Marcus Aurelius would laugh at him. Imagine, a Roman emperor in charge of a huge slice of the entire civilized world was as calm a man that ever existed. If an emperor could shrug it off why couldn't Riley?

He intellectually knew that he could leave this life at a moment's notice without the least misgiving. He'd done what he could. It wasn't great, nor measly. He used his inner and outer tools as well as he could. He'd be able to look anyone in the eye without blinking.

But then why was he so easily rattled? Emotionally shaky. Spinoza claimed that human nature, if there was such a thing, was governed (or misgoverned) by feelings, not reason. This wasn't the way it was supposed to be, but how it is. Riley didn't want to agree. But he was tempted.

The body was more powerful than the mind, even if the mind was regarded as the token ruler. A mere figurehead, perhaps. The real power resided in the muscles, nerves, blood cells, and DNA, and neurons. He couldn't win any fight against his flesh. The spirit eventually caved in to the truth.

Riley never stopped trying to form an alliance with his body. A useful partnership. With neither the mind dominating the body, or the body dominating the mind. Having them function as a team pointing toward the same goal.

The body seemed particularly strong and effective when the mind more or less stepped aside momentarily. When, say, an athlete was in their zone. When they did what they do best without the mind needlessly interfering and getting in the way.

But when the body tried to encroach on the mind's sector of responsibility it looked childish and weak. It was ridiculous when it squirmed and jumped around in an argument, as if it was touched with a cattle prod.

Passionate arguments were a losing tactic. Passion is better off displaying its gifts on a basketball court, or in a bedroom making love. Out of place in a serious debate. Vehement, hand-wringing emotional pleading is a sign of weakness when a person is trying to make a logical point. It's obviously the wrong approach.

He once again returned to the attack. The painting was slowly yielding to his desperate actions. The colors were better, in the sense that they weren't that popular. But he still cut back on the amount of colors he used. Orange, black, ivory, grey. That's plenty. Not strictly original, but a little more inventive.

Colors are like musical notes. Only a few exist, but what a range their combination can evoke. It's good not to settle into rigid patterns. He kept varying the mixtures. Some were better than others. He emphasized those blends in the future and phased out less desirable ones.

The plumbing crew hit him with some new problems. At this point he just acquiesced and had them proceed.

Also, the people in the front room weren't quite as stylish as he had hoped. One half was just littered with junk. Possessions, too many of the wrong kind. No order whatever, since another couple was only using it for storage at this point. But they couldn't make it any worse than the previous neighbors who occupied for a few years. Little by little the building was actually improved. At least it hadn't tumbled down on Riley's pathetic skull.

A realtor wanted to know if Riley was interested is selling it.

No, his old friend and mentor, Knute, had told him to never sell. Always buy more property. "If I live long enough I'll own the world!"

Riley had no dreams of owning the world. He wasn't sure he valued the world that much. It had its magnificent moments, but these were far and few between. Most of the time it wasn't much more than a pile of rubble strewn about at random.

Was this how he really felt, or was he merely adopting the pose of a cranky ancient philosopher? It was hard to say, but no one cared in the least about his attitude towards this earth. Love it and leave it. This was more like the truth of his permanent viewpoint.

Yeah. Planet earth: love it as much as you can, and then leave as soon as you're able. No matter what takes place after that you'll handle it with ease.

Although he refused to have a tombstone, if he did, it would say simply, his name followed underneath with these words: Love It and Leave it.

One of the zen riddles that Riley and Kristina enjoyed was a conversation between a zen abbot and a king. The king asked the monk "what happens after you die?" The zen master answered "I don't know. I haven't died."

Now, why didn't Riley think of that earthy reply? So simple, and commonsensical.

The painting was done. It might have been a step back instead of a leap forward. But at least it was an attractive move. What good is a leap forward if you only land in a pile of shit? You'd be better off retracing your steps and building up to another well-prepared leap. Who knows how that may turn out?

He'd clean up and walk over to Kristina's house for dinner. Chloe was coming. He hadn't seen her for a few weeks. She'd have plenty of stories about her latest job. Taking care of an old maniac for several weeks. To make sure she doesn't overdose on drugs.

Kristina had owned her California Craftsman style house for nearly a year. There was still work to be done on the large home. Riley was embarrassed that he didn't have the energy to do much of it himself. His studio took up most of his attention. The plumbing problems were on his mind as he sat down at his daughter's. He looked with approval at the chair she had reupholstered. Francisco, the upholsterer, was a neighbor. His shop was a block away on Whittier, and he also owned property on Oregon.

"He wants to go back to Mexico," Kristina said. He was getting older, had a sprawling family in both countries, and was thinking of returning to his native land. To die? Maybe that's what happens. You want to die where you were born.

Riley asked himself if he wanted to die in Iowa. He didn't see any reason to haul himself back to the Midwest just to croak. He'd be contented dying in his studio, painting and writing until the last moment. He wasn't sentimental about things like that. Dying is really a very private act. Like sitting on the toilet.

The chair was beautifully renewed. The golden leather flawless, and Francisco used "extra special foam", giving the cushions an excellent firmness.

"I have so much art in my home, but I could use some really good furniture. A piece or two, besides my tables," she said. Now she has one. A Midcentury, molded plywood, leather upholstered, recliner.

"This maniacal woman must exhaust you," Riley said to Chloe.

"She does. She won't even let any other person relieve me."

Chloe is a kind of therapist, a "sober companion", and watchdog for these out-of-control types becoming more numerous in Los Angeles.

"But it's expensive to have someone keeping an eye on you day and night. How does she pay for it?" Kristina asked.

"Her son is rich. He's a producer at Disney."

Usually Chloe deals with young men and women from wealthy families who've allowed themselves to be strung out on dope or booze. There's not a whole lot you can do if someone is determined to destroy themselves. Chloe manages to keep most of them alive. Not all of them. At a huge cost to their families. Today, however, it's an older woman.

"She jumps up and suggests things to do. The other day I had to take her shopping. She found this hat to buy. You know the one in Dr. Seuss. The Cat in the Hat. It's very tall and colorful. She was wearing it. I drove. We turned up the radio full blast to a classical music station, and had the windows rolled down. Her face is covered in gobs of makeup.

Like war paint. We stopped at a light, and this man next to us just stared, and finally took a snapshot on his phone."

"I guess that's what a son does these days if he has a crazy mother. And he has enough money to hire someone to put her on a leash. Maybe it's always been that way."

Riley knew so little about these things. His life had been devoted to his art, and some romantic episodes. But a lot of people had more problems than that to deal with. How would he be able to paint if he had to be a nurse to a batty mother? He was luckier than he realized.

But Chloe was a writer, and this role is a bonanza for her.

"I write two pages every day," she said. "In my journal. But once I left it open and the woman saw it and asked if I was taking notes. I quickly grabbed the booklet and put it in the car and locked the door. If she found it I'd be out of a job."

"That's the stuff I worry about. But what about your stories based the on the girl who ended up dying?"

"I finished that."

"How many pages is it?"

"Oh, it's a stack of them. A whole book. I sent it off to my agent in London."

"And what did he think of it?"

"He wrote and said it was a powerful ending. I still need a title."

"Chloe, that's the best news. And you're still publishing your short stories?"

"I am. I sent two out to this one magazine. The editor likes the stories and prints them, so I may as well send them to him."

"Do you have any idea of how many you've published?"

"No. I haven't."

"Do people ever ask you about that? I mean people you meet, or those in your writing class."

"Not people in the class, since they're older and published, but other people do ask."

"They must be impressed."

Chloe didn't exactly blush. She handled the compliment from her step-father like a pro, which she is.

They were sitting at the slab table, sharing chicken and a pizza. Riley had his red wine. He wouldn't eat dinner without it. They understood, although no one else drank.

"I'm thinking of giving Philippe a call," said Kristina. "But I feel a little shy about it."

"You haven't heard from him?"

"Not since he wrote about reading your novel."

"You never wrote back?"

"No."

"Well, in that case. Why not answer him?"

Riley wondered how the European guy who went out with Kristina a month ago, thought about his book. He must have something to say, since one of the characters resembled him.

Plus he sensed that his daughter enjoyed video chatting with him.

"I think the three of us are shy. We never pursue anyone. And if we get the slightest hint that they might be rejecting us we're gone forever."

"That's true. I can't imagine begging some guy. It's an appalling idea."

They all agreed with that position.

"But I guess a person isn't shy if they say 'I'm shy.'"

"No, that would be proof they're bold."

"Shy is something other people say about you. Like beautiful."

Riley listened as the daughters discussed the men who live in the Valley.

"But you've never dated one," said Kristina.

"I haven't."

"I have. It's not something I want to do again."

"Because of the Valley?"

"It's not that. But it isn't for me."

"I think I understand."

The talk continued. Raphael ran up to his room. It was a family night.

It was good, but the three adults all felt the difference between a thrilling night and a family night.

Not that it was bad. No, there were many that were much worse. They all wondered if this feeling was a mature, grounded one, or something more like a holding pattern. Like a plane circling in the air, waiting to land.

It was neither hell nor heaven. And certainly not purgatory, or some painful layover.

It had a feeling of relief. Of escape from dark places. Suffocating traps. And it also felt somewhat triumphant. That they've all three mastered a difficult environment.

"I used to see people who looked sort of blase. Or maybe just preoccupied, and compared to me, stabilized, with their feet on the ground. And I suspected that they were people who have lived in Los Angeles for many years. They'd already gone through the various phases. The excitement, the hopes, the taste of a surprising success, even a moment of what might pass as fame, a type of fame that never really got any bigger, and quickly vanished. They were farther along in this world. And maybe we've turned into those people."

"But you have to have lived it."

"You can't fake it. Experience can't be bought, traded, or given away as a present."

Whatever it is he was feeling it was a major improvement on anything from his previous times. Nothing back there was equal to his present reality.

Los Angeles

September, 2019

About the author:

Patrick McCarthy is a fulltime artist living in Los Angeles. He graduated from U. of Notre Dame with a B. A., and U. of Missouri with an M. A.

This is his twenty-first novel. They can be purchased on Amazon.

His Instagram page is Pfm77.

Email: Pfm7

Printed in Great
Britain
by Amazon